Purrfectly Caught

A MAVERICK PRIDE TALE

THE MAVERICK PRIDE TALES
BOOK FOUR

C.D. GORRI

Purrfectly Caught:
A Maverick Pride Tale 4
by C.D. Gorri
Edited by BookNookNuts

Dear readers,
May all your dreams come true.

Before you begin sign up for my newsletter here:
https://www.cdgorri.com/newsletter

Blurb

She is determined to live alone. He won't take no for an answer.

Moving to a new town isn't easy, but Kylie McNaughton is determined to get away from her old South Carolina Pride. When she's accepted by the Neta of Maverick Point, it's almost too good to be true. Finally, she can just live in peace and lose herself in her designs.

Never mind the gorgeous male who gives her goosebumps every time he is near. Kylie doesn't have time for a mate. Things heat up when the persistent Tiger refuses to take no for an answer.

Michael Turner is the Pride Healer and one of the Neta's own Honor Guard. His Tiger is positive the curvy blonde Shifter is his mate, but she runs every time she sees him!

Flabbergasted by her behavior, he is ready to throw in the towel. But when Uncle Uzzi comes to visit with bad tidings from the Shifter Council, it seems Kylie's old Pride wants her returned to them. Now.

Mikey is forced to make a decision that puts him at odds with the blonde beauty, but it's just what he needs to catch the curvy female.

Will an old enemy break up the newly mated pair?

Welcome to Uncle Uzzi's Magical Matchmaking Service!

The breeze coming off the Atlantic was chilly, but Uzzi Stregovich kept his window open. Hank, his driver, did not mind the cold in the least. Shifters usually didn't.

Stomach growling, he looked down at the box of goodies Richard, his housekeeper who came in once a week to cook for the old Witch, had baked a special apple cake especially for this trip.

Of course, he shouldn't steal a slice before he arrived. That would be rude, and his beloved wife, Betty, would never tolerate rudeness from her husband.

"I know, *liebling*, I will wait for Elissa and Hunter before I take a piece," he whispered, in case her spirit hovered near.

He always felt her presence surrounding him like the warm summer sun, peaceful and serene, and Uzzi could not wait for the day they would be together again. Alas, it would be some time yet, but in the meantime, Uzzi would not ignore his calling.

His Magic danced and buzzed along his skin, and he was certain this trip would be fruitful. Going on eighty-four years now, the Witch had been finding fated pairs and bringing them together. Even in the supernatural world, his was truly a unique calling.

As a descendant of the Goddess of Love herself, Uzzi's special talents were best served finding mates that had been fated to be together before even time began. He had been lucky to find his own soul in his sweet Betty, and she had helped him keep his vow to bring others the same joy.

Uncle Uzzi's Matchmaking Service was not altogether perfect, more like a tool the Universe employed to its own ends. Uzzi was fine with that. He preferred to work with the ever-present, powerful forces that moved through time and space.

It was better for business, and for his clients that way. His next project involved his favorite Tiger Pride, of course, which was why he was on his way back to Maverick Point.

"I have to stop for gas," Hank told him, and Uzzi smiled.

"Excellent. I believe the station coming up has fine coffee," he remarked, blue eyes twinkling with delight. He did so enjoy a good cup of joe!

Uncle Uzzi was going to need the extra jolt of caffeine to help this next fated pair.

Prologue

T he wind stopped howling, and the sudden stillness was almost eerie. As if it too sensed the coming of something big, something unstoppable.

Michael stalked through the tall trees, moving silently over the stubby grass, groundcover, and shrubs that dotted the woods that ran behind the center of town where most of the local shops and restaurants were located.

Maverick Point was a touch more rural than many of the cities and suburbs that made up the Garden State. Not too crowded, but close enough to the city to make a day trip of it. He liked it that way, and so did his beast.

Of course, he was not supposed to be in town

just then. Oh no, Michael had duties that required him to be back at the Pride House, watching over the very pregnant and very irritable Nari, their title for Alpha female.

Bengal Tiger Shifter culture, though completely Americanized, was still rooted in the old world. A lot of their terms came from Bangla words and phrases, most of which he'd learned as a cub, along with English, French, Italian, and a little Sioux, at the foot of his grandmother who'd raised him. Shifters had an ear for languages and accents.

His ears twitched, anticipating hearing the little blonde that he was currently stalking. She had the most undeniably sweet Southern twang, though she did her best to hide it. Wasn't easy to do that in a Pride, but no one called her out on it, which was good. Michael had never been one to cause trouble, but he already knew that anyone who gave the sweet little she-Cat a hard time would have to deal with him.

So yes, it was very good his Pride mates seemed to welcome the petite female and bring her immediately into the fold. Otherwise, his beast would've had a lot to say about that. Chuffing softly, he tested the air, looking for any hint she'd come this way.

Fuck. What am I doing?

The answer was easy. It was the same thing he'd been doing daily since she'd come to town. Pathetic, and he knew it. But he had no choice.

Michael was all nerves these days. He could hardly sleep anymore, tossing and turning through all hours of the night had become more than habit. It was like a torturous ritual.

After his rounds at the clinic, he'd given his daily report to the Neta, then went to check on the Nari's health and comfort. Elissa was a former normal who'd undergone the *Puspa* and was now a Tiger Shifter like the rest of them.

The Pride had rejoiced heartily that the Universe had blessed the union of Hunter and Elissa by deeming her worthy of the Puspa. The magical change that had transformed her from human to Shifter after receiving the claiming bite of her fated mate was rare and coveted, and now another mate had gone through the change as well.

The Maverick Pride was booming with mates, and soon a new line of cubs would be born, increasing the Pride's strength and size. Nothing so glorious as the offspring of mated pairs. Those cubs born to true lovers were wanted and happy, raised with love and protected by all. Shifters so rarely produced viable young that each cub was looked after and regarded by all as family.

As a doctor and Pride Healer, Michael was keenly aware of that not so small fact. He was both curious and a little worried about the Nari's pregnancy, as was her mate. The big as fuck, and twice as scary, Neta was a tad overprotective.

Hunter was not a bad man, he was just a wee bit on edge. Michael knew the feeling. His Tiger growled impatiently as they hurried to their final destination.

What the hell am I doing here?

He repeated the question from within the metaphysical realm where his human half waited while he ran in his fur. The woman did not want to see him. She had made that abundantly clear over the past few months.

And yet, there he was. She had him wound so tightly he was taking runs twice daily. Just to catch a glimpse of his heart's own desire.

So great was his need to see *her*, that his patient, the rather *impatient* Elissa Maverick, had kicked him out of the Pride House.

"I swear to God, Mikey, if you don't stop pacing, I'm going to tear you a new asshole! Just tell the woman how you feel. Go on! Get the heck out of here before I sic

Hunter on you," the Nari had threatened before pushing him out the door.

Literally.

Fuck, the woman had gotten even stronger in her "delicate" condition. His beast groaned at the indignity of it all. A big bad Tiger, like him, being shoved around by the tiny female was preposterous.

And yet it happened, chuffed his Tiger.

Michael would never want to upset Elissa. The female was the cherished mate of his Neta, and in her condition, she was valued and loved by the entire Pride.

His beast snorted, as close to actual laughter as his Tiger could come. Still, this was a serious matter. Shifter pregnancies were typically complicated. The sad truth was they rarely came to fruition.

The birthing of viable Shifter young was unfortunately not the norm. That went for all Shifter-kind. It was why mating with humans was so keenly advised.

The same inherent magic that made it possible for beings to have dual natures also made it singularly difficult to carry and deliver to term.

Elissa was special in more ways than one. Not only was she the true and fated mate of Hunter Maverick, Pride Neta, but because she had experienced the *Puspa,* it was believed she would bring a sort of fertile healing to the Pride.

To Tiger Shifters, there was no greater honor. With his claiming bite, Hunter had given Elissa the ability to change into a beast of her own. The fact her other form was a beautiful white Tiger, rare indeed, just leant more credence to what was fast becoming her legend.

Hunter and Elissa were the Pride's own fairytale couple. Michael, and the others of the Guard, knew they were all too real. But they too had marveled at the exceedingly rare gift the Fates had granted their Pride.

It seemed the Tigers of the Maverick Pride were blessed when it came to finding and wooing their fated mates.

Except for me, his beast snarled at the thought.

Michael understood the Fates had given his Pride a most worthy honor in finding their true mates using *Uncle Uzzi's Magical Matchmaking Services.* The old Witch seemed Heaven sent to many of them.

And yet, it was nigh impossible for him to obtain his own happily ever after. Pain speared his heart and his beast growled softly.

What the heck had he done to piss the Fates off, anyway?

Michael wished he could simply call Uncle Uzzi and have him find his fated mate, but what good would that do?

The guess work had been taken out of the equation. He knew who she was and where, but the female simply was not interested. Once more, he felt a pain slice through him at the thought. So strong, it threatened to send him to his knees, and would have had he been in human form.

This was futile! Coming here to try to steal a peek at her. Michael had a sacred duty as Pride Healer to attend his Nari, but she was right to cast him out. He was no good to her if he was this amped up.

Elissa was due any day now, but it was just too damn difficult for him to concentrate. A problem for sure, and one he'd developed immediately after setting his eyes on a certain curvy goddess.

Kylie, her name whispered through his mind and his beast growled softly in his throat. *Why don't you want me?*

Kylie McNaughton was an enigma to him. Man and beast had recognized her immediately as his and he had been dying to sink his teeth into her soft flesh ever since he'd first met the tiny blonde.

Of course, the petite beauty had been avoiding

him just as long. The one time he'd actually touched her, she'd been injured defending the Nari from a streak of rogue Tigers who had been grossly misguided by the Maverick Pride's former, and now deceased Beta, Blake.

If the Neta had not taken him out, Mikey would have for that infraction alone. Seeing her pale skin marred by scratches and bruises had damn near driven him mad with bloodlust.

It was all Brayden, the Pride Beta, and Hunter, could do to stop him from killing the remaining streak Tigers, who they took as prisoners until the Council had come to retrieve them.

Stupid cubs had been manipulated by a madman, but to Mikey, their actions were unforgiveable.

They later learned that Blake's misdeeds had been farther reaching than they'd imagined. The female population and the youth of the Pride had suffered greatly at his bloodied hands, unbeknownst to Hunter, and the rest of his most trusted Pride mates. A problem they were currently seeking solutions to.

His Tiger paced unhappily at the thought of Kylie's bruised and battered body after her attack. She'd lost a lot of blood during that battle, and her wounds had been many. Still, he could not help but be proud of her. The fierce she-Tiger had fought so bravely.

More so than he'd have given her credit for, but the bruises and breaks on her assailants had attested to that fact. The women had done well.

Even he would have had a hard time fighting off so many Shifter males. Her bravery and fighting skills were truly great. A medical man, he abhorred violence on principal, but as a Shifter he understood the need, and had himself been carried away by bloodlust a time or two.

Complexities made them human. That, and their hopes, dreams, desires, and ability to change their minds. To learn and grow, to feel and appreciate, and to sit around mooning for a female who did not even care that he was alive, apparently.

Fuck and damn.

Michael had treated Kylie's wounds and dressed her breaks. He'd carried her to her apartment afterwards, and yes, he'd sat with her throughout the night, tending her every need. His Tiger had been damn near crazy with worry by the time she'd opened her beautiful green eyes.

The unusual color was one of the first things that had attracted him to the tiny woman. They were pale and crystalline, like looking through little drops of dew atop tiny spring buds that had yet to bloom.

More celery than emerald in color, he supposed, but he was not an artist. He had no idea what else to compare it to. All he knew was he loved her eyes.

That night, he'd blessed the day he'd decided to apprentice his grandmother. As the former Pride Healer, she taught him many things. That knowledge allowed him to look after Kylie in her hour of need, satisfying a primal urge inside of him to care for her.

Mate, chuffed his beast.

Shit. His need for her was growing daily, but he had no idea how to make her listen. Where was his grandmother now that he needed advice on how to woo his woman?

Retired to Florida, spending the rest of her days playing golf and sipping *Mai Tais* he supposed with a snort. Her old bones couldn't take the cold anymore, or so she'd said. Still, he missed her. Very much.

Nana Turner had raised him after his own mother had left town. A *normal*, his mother had decided she wasn't cut out for Pride life after her mate had passed.

He bore her no ill will. It had been for the best, he supposed. Unconventional and smart-mouthed, his grandmother had prepared him for a great many things, but not this.

Nothing could've prepared him for the pained feeling of wanting his mate and knowing he had no idea how to get her.

His attention was caught by a light switching on in the apartment just over *Jessica's Closet*. That was her.

Kylie, he thought, and listened for any sign of what she was doing.

There.

He followed the sound of her footsteps as she moved unhurriedly from one room to the other. The slide of the balcony door opening was loud in his ears, but he remained still and unmoving. Waiting for the moment when she finally emerged.

Kylie was a creature of habit, at least as far as he'd been able to discover for himself. For whatever reason, his unclaimed mate liked to sit in the early morning darkness with her coffee, all alone.

Maybe she was thinking deep thoughts, or maybe she was simply taking in the air. He could only wonder. Once or twice he thought she'd seen him, but he couldn't know for certain.

He was a patient man, but even Michael had his

breaking point. Sooner or later he'd be scaling that balcony and taking what was his.

Ready or not, he had plans to catch a certain little kitten. And he was prepared to use every tool he had.

Mine.

Chapter One

Uncle Uzzi sipped his coffee before calmly retrieving his cell phone from where he sat in the back of the limo.

The summer morning was just starting to warm under that bright ball of fire in the sky. He smiled, happy he had left the windows rolled down.

It had been chilly when they'd started driving down from Cape Cod, where he had been away on business. Uzzi was quite the traveler. He had to be in order to bring his services where they were needed.

Regardless of the outside temperature, he was always comfortable in his light pants and sweater. His wife had said his sense of fashion was limited, but he never cared so long as he was comfortable. How he missed her, he thought and sighed.

"Yes, this is Uncle Uzzi," he said with a knowing smile on his face.

"Of course," Uzzi sat a little straighter in his seat, his smile turning down.

So this was why his magic had been acting up, so insistent he return to the Pride, he thought with a frown.

"Right. Well, it is good you called me. I think I can help sort this out for you. I will be in touch soon," he returned, and thought for a moment before dialing.

This situation was rare and troubling. He had thought he would have more time to deal with it, but there were always so many moving parts, a poor Witch like Uzzi could hardly be blamed for not seeing them all. Besides, the Fates enjoyed their little games.

"You alright, Uncle Uzzi?" Hank's keen eyes met his in the rearview mirror.

How he loved that boy! Hank was his own honorary nephew, he thought and nodded, raising a finger to indicate he would reply in only a moment.

"Hunter? Uncle Uzzi here," he said.

"Yes, indeed. I am afraid I have to speak with you about one of your Pride members," he continued. "In person would be best. I am on my way now, as you know I was already coming down for Elissa's baby shower, but tell me, can you put up with me for an extra night or two?" he asked, laughing at Hunter's reply, then went on.

"Thank you, yes, I will see you then."

Hmm.

He had been working with the Tiger Shifters of Maverick Point for the better part of a year now, but this was by far the strangest case he had ever had.

It was going to be tricky.

But---with a little perseverance---he just might be able to pull it off! How could he not? Uzzi wanted to help these two souls come together, after all, it was his job. They were meant to be, even if stubbornness was getting in the way.

More importantly, his manipulations could very well stop a tragedy from occurring. Determined to do whatever he could, Uzzi turned to Hank.

"Better step on it, Hank. I am afraid the situation is dire."

"Yes, sir," Hank replied, and grinned. He always did enjoy going over the speed limits.

Well, thought Uzzi, *it looks like another pussy is about to bite the dust.*

He grinned wickedly at his little joke, closing his eyes as his magic pulsed and swelled.

Maverick Point was just another hour or so away, and he needed to focus his magic on the upcoming task. Uzzi closed his eyes and began to hum, calling his powers to him so he might read more of the future to determine the correct path.

This pair was going to be a little trickier than the last, but as always, Uncle Uzzi trusted in the universe and in himself.

He knew what had to be done.

*B*ack in Maverick Point...

"Kylie! Did you remember the little sachets with the Jordan almonds?"

Kylie rolled her eyes playfully at Gretchen, while Jessica continued to boss both of them around. Not that she could blame the redheaded she-Tiger. It was their Nari's baby shower, and *everyone* was doing their part to pitch in. Even the still too skinny, and somewhat bitchy, Pamela Brown was helping out.

The woman was apparently awesome with a *Cricut* and had volunteered to make little pink and blue labels with "Baby Maverick" in a wonderfully curly font for all the invitations and thank you cards.

"Yes, Jessica, even though I can't tell why anyone

would want to eat the little tooth-breakers, the almond goody bags are done," Kylie replied, absently rubbing her jaw while she thought about her last encounter with the unpleasantly hard, candied nuts.

"I told you why I wanted them," Jessica began. "Elissa and Hunter didn't get to have a traditional wedding, and with her background, I wanted to do something special for them and their new cub."

"Yeah, you said that. But why couldn't we use gummies or chocolates?" she asked, waiting for Jessica to continue her explanation.

"No! That wouldn't work. Elissa's Italian heritage comes from her grandmother, who raised her. Jordan almonds are traditional. And you know, her grandmother meant a lot to our Nari," Jess said. "And I know that tradition means a lot to Elissa. Anyway, I did some research," Jess added excitedly.

"Well, are you going to keep us waiting, *heifer?*" Gretchen asked, sticking her tongue out at Jessica.

"Pfbbbt!" Jessica blew a raspberry at Gretch. "I'm not talking to you. I'm talking to Kylie. *Fuck you very much.*"

"You are such a *beyotch,*" Gretchen teased in a horribly off key sing-song voice.

Kylie was tempted to giggle, but she knew all too well what would happen if she didn't get Jessica back on track. And she so did not have time to clean up another one of their food fights or wrestling matches.

Sigh.

Having girlfriends who were also Shifters was such a chore sometimes, she thought, grinning widely.

She was not being honest, though. Fact was, Kylie loved these beyotches. She'd never had close friends growing up, but this was more than making up for it.

"Gretchen, please hush up. Now Jessica, before I get madder than a wet hen---would you please get a move on with this story, girl?"

"Okay, where was I? Oh yeah!" Jess smiled.

"In a traditional Italian wedding, Jordan almonds are given to the guests to remind them of both the bitterness and sweetness of married life. Specifically, five almonds are given to represent happiness, health, wealth, longevity, and fertility."

"Well, Hunter and Elissa pretty much have all that already. I say we go with the chocolates," Gretchen replied with an extra side of snark.

This time, Kylie hid her smirk from Jessica's narrow-eyed glare. She knew the woman meant well, but it was a little over the top, even for her. But knowing it all came from a good place made Kylie more than happy to do her part for the Alpha couple, who had welcomed her with open arms into their Pride.

Truth was, she'd never known anything like it. Had never seen that level of loyalty, trust, respect, and love within a Shifter group. Certainly not where she'd been raised.

That kind of overall goodwill did not exist in the Sharp Claw Pride.

Kylie shivered, pushing the hurtful memories back as they threatened to rise and sour her mood altogether.

Not now, she told herself sternly.

This was a happy time. A time of friendship and new beginnings. Her website had just gotten its hundred-thousandth follower, and she had standing orders from local retailers for her *Kisses by Kylie* line, and more coming in everyday.

"Okay, ladies, what do y'all think about my gift?" she asked, a little of her Southern accent sneaking out unintentionally with her words.

"Awww! I love it when you say *y'all*," gushed Jessica, completely unaware of Kylie's pinking cheeks.

Mostly, Kylie had acclimated to the Northeastern state's particular lack of the usage of the word *y'all*, but now and then, it snuck up on her. She shook off the discomfort of being the center of attention and turned the conversation back to her original question. Knowing in her heart the other she-Tiger was not being condescending in any way really helped with that.

"Oh hush," she muttered, lifting what she'd created with the Nari in mind. "I made Elissa six luxury nursing bra and panty sets, with matching robes and slipper socks."

She held up the pastel colored confections and knew her cheeks were positively pink with how warm she felt. Being a successful designer meant having a thick skin when it came to critics, but it also meant pushing beyond her comfort zone and getting out there to show her stuff.

"*OMG!* Those are so pretty, Kylie. Elissa is going to love them," Jessica exclaimed, and Kylie beamed under the praise.

"Well, I'm hoping she will," she confessed, and her cheeks burned even more as she worked up enough courage to bring up the next part of her announcement. "You see, these are going to be the highlight of my new *Mommies By Kylie* line. What do y'all think?"

Watching their reactions with bated breath, she immediately exhaled when both women applauded, and wolf whistled. Kylie barked a short laugh.

"I want some too!" Jessica whined.

"You need some," Gretchen said, before the two of them started throwing tissue paper at each other.

Ignoring their shenanigans, Kylie refolded the sets and wrapped them carefully in the large gift box she had ordered just for the Nari. It was printed with black velvety tiger stripes on top of a glossy white background, and the interior tissue paper matched.

Kylie had worked especially hard on this new project, researching which fabrics were breathable and promoted healthy milk production and comfort for mother and babe. Plus, she wanted them to be cute. New moms deserved to look good too, and it would not hurt to boost their confidence, in Kylie's humble opinion.

The nursing bras currently available on the market were exactly like the ones her grandmother wore. Of course, that was code for *functional* and *ugly as fuck.*

Then there was the other problem. A bigger problem, so to speak. The damn things never seemed to fit correctly. It was a serious issue, especially for the curvier than was deemed trendy new mom. And on the rare and unique experience of finding a nursing bra that was pretty and the correct size, it could potentially cost upwards of several hundred dollars.

Hardly affordable, and definitely not acceptable to Kylie. She wanted to change that. Nursing bras were a necessity, and everyone, regardless of size, shape and bank account, should have several options.

So, she'd done the research and had finally come up with a concept where the nursing mother could simply unclip the outer shell of the bra, and pull the material down to feed her baby, without suffocating the tiny boy or girl while maintaining a light and comfortable, totally workable, design.

Unlike the bulky, hard plastic connectors used by her competitors, Kylie employed a simple wire hook and eye that she'd wrapped in organic cotton thread to be soft to the touch. Simplicity was key.

As with most things, she found modern manufacturers and designers were always looking for new, easy, and cheap. They had forgotten that simplicity with taste was best of all.

Her *Mommies By Kylie* line would hopefully fill a hole in the market. She was using the best environmentally sustainable materials, like organic cotton, bamboo, and micro-jersey fabrics, and making them pretty with either scalloped lace, satin, silk, and tulle trim.

Her designs were modern and comfortable, offering new mothers style and durability with functionality. And again, there was the pretty factor.

For Elissa, she'd used various shades of nude, pale pinks, sage greens, and ocean blues to complete her collection. The Nari would be her guinea pig, *er*, Tiger, and she could not wait to see how she liked them.

"You have to let me sell these in my store. And who knows, maybe I will be buying a few for myself sooner than later," Jessica said after dumping an entire box full of biodegradable packing peanuts on Gretchen's multi-colored head.

"Oh my Lord! Jess, I was hoping you would say that," she told her boss and exhaled.

Once more, she was grateful for her friend's willingness to showcase her creations.

"Wait! Do you mean it? You're pregnant?" Kylie asked, and the redhead blushed an alarming shade of pink.

"What? OMG! You are? Why did you let me tease you like that? Shit! Don't touch me, it might be contagious," Gretchen shrieked and raced away from Jessica to Kylie's side.

"The way you and Reg go at it? Hell yes, it's contagious. Congrats, Jess honey," Kylie answered, tsking at Gretchen who was trying not to laugh as they both embraced Jessica.

"Thank you. We haven't told anyone else yet," she said. "We wanted to wait until after Elissa has hers."

"That is really thoughtful of you," Gretchen replied and kissed Jessica's cheek.

"It is," Kylie added. "Anyway, here you go. I made a hundred bags of those terrible candies, even though we are keeping it small," she handed a box full of the pretty Jordan almond party favors.

They were tied closed with little pink and blue ribbons that had "Baby Maverick" printed on them courtesy of Pamela. The woman had dropped them off the day before with hardly a word to Kylie.

Whatever.

Chapter Two

S he might have turned a new leaf, but she was still skating on thin ice far as Kylie, and her inner she-Tiger, was concerned.

"They're perfect," gushed Jessica. "Brayden texted to say the tent is all set up, and the karaoke machine---"

Kylie whipped her head towards Jess first, then Gretchen. Her blonde hair landed in her face as she spun around to confront the females. Lying heifers!

"I thought we weren't doing *that*," Kylie sputtered, dreading the inevitable.

Since their Nari was expecting, and could no longer partake in *Wine Wednesdays*, which had become a little ritual amongst the female members of the Pride, they'd done something Kylie had dreaded every week since.

They had bought the woman a karaoke machine. *Wine Wednesdays* had quickly become *Whine Wednesdays* since, unfortunately, most of the Pride females could not carry a damn tune. So far, Kylie had managed to avoid singing with those crazy beyotches, but that was because she always made sure to bring some new project she was working on.

Luckily, the ladies of the Pride were only too glad not to interrupt her work. After all, she offered a 25% discount to Pride members on all of her lingerie sets and separates.

"Well, it's just in case Elissa feels like it. You know, you could have joined in on last week's *Girls Just Wanna Have Fun* rendition," Jessica added.

"Not if I wanted to keep my hearing intact," Kylie mumbled, but it was no good. Both women were Shifters and could hear her just fine.

"Anyway," Jessica said, sticking her tongue out at Kylie before continuing. "The tent is up, we just have to decorate it, and keep the guest of honor away until the party starts."

"I am on it. My kit is all packed with goodies. I'm going to give her a mani-pedi, a facial, and a prenatal massage. Then I am going to cut her hair and follow it up with this wonderful argan oil, mint, and honey conditioning treatment. Mama Elissa is gonna get some real pampering," Gretchen said, and Kylie high-fived her.

"Who's going to watch *Cut It Out* for you?" Jess asked.

"I left Marion in charge."

"Good idea. He did a great job with my highlights the other day," Kylie offered.

"Yeah, he's the best. Anyway, he is loving that he gets to train our newest hire, Ms. Pamela Brown, herself," Gretchen announced.

Kylie stopped in her tracks and looked at her friend. Did she hear her correctly? She couldn't be serious. Pamela Brown was a first-class bitch.

It was one thing to let her make some labels and bows, but another to have her underfoot all the time. That sneaky little she-Tiger had tried to set a trap to hurt Gretchen only a few months ago.

"Before you say anything," Gretchen began, holding up her hand to stop Jess and Kylie from interrupting.

It was all Kylie could do not to walk over there and shake her new bestie. Friends were hard to come by, or at least, they were for her. So, maybe she was a *teeny weeny* bit overprotective.

"I love that you both wanna protect me, but there is no need. I'm a Tiger now, remember? Anyway, she's changed. I swear it," Gretchen replied earnestly.

"Gretch, are you sure?"

"Yes, I am. Look, Pamela is a different woman now, or at least she is trying to be. I mean, look, she was manipulated and abused at the hands of someone who was in a position of power over her, who she trusted. Everyone did, right? I mean, Blake was the Beta."

"Yes, he was," Jessica agreed, and huffed out an annoyed breath.

The unfortunate events had happened right around the time Kylie had arrived in Maverick Point. The turn of events was what convinced her to ask permission to join the Pride. Hunter was a powerful Neta, and he was fair, too.

He did not cower under the pressure of having the man he was supposed to trust the most, his own Beta, try to usurp him and steal his position. Hunter Maverick had met that poisonous weasel head on.

Once the worthless man had attacked his mate, Hunter did what he had to. He'd ended his life and protected his own mate, and the Pride as a whole. It was that kind of strength and resolve to fight injustice that made Kylie want to make a home in Maverick Point.

"I mean, thank goodness he's dead and all, but the havoc he'd wreaked before his fortunate demise was beyond damaging," Gretchen explained.

"I can't argue with that," Jessica agreed.

"Anyway, Reg and I have been working with Hunter on a plan, and well, I was thinking a support group. You know, like a safe place for them to come and share stories so they don't feel so alone. Maybe we can help them find ways to get rid of the taint or tarnish they feel as a result of what happened. It would be open to all, but especially for those in the Pride who'd been victimized by Blake and his associates. Well? Thoughts?"

There was a pregnant pause, and Kylie frowned. She should have known better than to sling judgment on others. Hadn't she been cruelly treated to such hostile opinions for most of her life?

Badly done, Kylie, she thought to herself.

"Wow, I'm such a shallow ass," Jess said, interrupting her own self-reproach. "I think it's awesome Gretchen. Anything we can do to help, well, you can just count me and Brayden in."

"Thank you," Gretchen replied, squeezing Jess' hand and smiling through tears. "Kylie? I don't expect you to have like sleepovers and pillow fights with Pam, but I mean, at the very least, she deserves the benefit of the doubt. Are you going to mind it very terribly that she works for me now?"

Kylie blinked, surprised this woman cared at all what she felt or thought. She was humbled by the friendship so readily offered by the females of the Maverick Pride. They had been nothing but welcoming and kind, supportive in her personal life, what they knew of it, and in her business.

She'd taken their friendship greedily too. Maybe it was time she paid it forward, the thought with a frown.

"I'm so sorry, Gretchen. I might need some time to adjust to her, but it's *your* shop. You don't need me to approve of your employees. It's just harder for me to forgive and to trust someone after they've been disloyal, but that is because of my own past and experiences. Now, that said, of course I will help you with whatever you need," Kylie replied and nodded her head.

She worried her lower lip between her teeth, thinking about things she was better off forgetting. Damn it. She hated when those thoughts crept in. People screaming, the blows that followed, and, of course, the pain. Always so much pain.

"You don't talk about your past much," Jessica interrupted almost casually, but Kylie knew phishing when she heard it. "I just want you to know we are here for you, if ever you need us."

"I know," Kylie said. "I'm just gonna grab the last of the decorations, then I'll follow you to the Pride House in my car."

"Okay." Jessica winked.

She and Gretchen grabbed boxes and bags and headed out to her SUV. They were all invested in this baby shower, and it had been so much fun to prepare for it all. Bonding with other women was so rare and precious a thing, she felt truly blessed for her time with these females.

Kylie was especially proud of the work she'd put into making Elissa's gift. Her line of lingerie was her key out of the poverty she'd been born into and her own independence. Plus, she really loved designing.

Whenever she sewed a new creation, it was as if all the problems she'd ever had simply slipped away. Kylie became absorbed in the colors and patterns and neat stitching. She could forget her past then.

Luckily, her inner muses were always on the go, or so it would seem. She smiled and picked up the huge tiger striped box holding all the tissue paper wrapped goodies she'd made Elissa, along with a dozen unisex burping clothes for the baby in her hands. She already had the bag of decorations slung on her shoulder next to her purse. Thank goodness she was a Shifter, she'd have needed superstrength just to lug everything outside.

She waited as Jess gave some last-minute instructions to the college girls who worked for her after classes and on the weekends. They were younger members of the Pride and proved themselves reliable. She waved keys in hand and asked them to lock up her work room.

The Fates had truly blessed her when she'd found the Maverick Pride. They'd taken her in with open arms and very few questions asked. Which was just how she liked it. If that meant she'd have to put up with the likes of Pamela, she could do it.

Especially since she knew it would ease her friend's mind once she did. Her inner she-Tiger chuffed at the mere mention of the nasty feline's name, but Kylie silenced her animal.

Being on the run for so long, she'd forgotten what it was like to have friends. Sometimes, you had to compromise, and there was nothing wrong with giving Pamela a chance, was there?

The militant Pride where she had grown up didn't exactly foster healthy relationships. Kylie shuddered as her mind wandered down the cold lane of her memories as she drove down the semi empty streets to the Pride House.

She could scarcely believe she used to live in one. A grand old thing, it was located on a former plantation that had been run by Shifters. The place always felt full of ghosts and memories to the much younger Kylie who'd never felt at home there.

A relic of times long gone and forgotten. Times, that for the sake of the Sharp Claw Pride, should have been remembered. Sadly, their Pride Keeper had died before Kylie had even been born. With him went the legacies of their violent and gory past.

Born of the Sharp Claw Pride House's bloody line, it was a wonder she was alive today and not legally insane. Vicious killings, miscarriages of justice, and brutality were what made up her lineage.

For fuck's sake, her own mother had tried to have her killed. Leaving had been a necessity. There was nothing else she could have done.

Sometimes, blood was just blood, and bad blood was best left behind.

Kylie sometimes recalled the males and females of the Pride, who had been kind to her as a cub. Some were good Shifters, but they were still stuck under her mother's rule.

Her heart hurt for them, and she prayed to the gods that they were okay more often than not. Kylie's worst fear, though, was that she would end up like her mother, in some small and hateful way.

She worried that she was somehow broken or malfunctioning as a woman, as a she-Tiger. Of course, she'd only ever admit that to herself.

As it was, she didn't tell anyone about the circumstances that had led to her leaving home, except for Hunter Maverick. As her new Neta, he had the right to know who and what he was inviting into his home.

It was not something she wanted to discuss with anyone else.

Like not ever.

The big bald man had simply looked at her with those piercing teal eyes of his. After a minute had passed---and Kylie had thought for sure that he had been about to kick her ass to the curb---he'd opened his lips and asked her one question.

"Do you wish to become part of our Pride? I ask you completely without pressure or expectation. You have leave to remain here as long as you want, under our protection either way," he'd stated.

"Yes, Neta. I would like to become one of the Pride,"

she'd responded, feeling like she belonged there for some unknown reason.

"Then, I welcome you, Kylie McNaughton, to the Maverick Pride. You are ours to protect, and you will guard in turn. We are not like your old Pride. I promise you that. Maverick Point is your home now and will remain a safe harbor for you always."

"Thank you, Neta."

It was only after he'd taken her forearm in his hand and pressed his head to hers that she'd felt the Pride bonds surround her in a way she had not experienced since the passing of her father.

Kylie missed the old man so much. He'd been kind and gentle. A loving man and nurturer, where her mother had lacked all maternal instinct.

She'd killed him before Kylie had her tenth birthday. Afterwards, she had known nothing but fear while she had lived under her mother's roof. The woman who'd birthed her seemed to hate Kylie right from the start.

She'd punished her often as a child, and once she'd had her first shift, the real cruelty had begun. Often in the form of sneak attacks and brutal displays of strength waged against her by stronger males.

All of it done for the sole enjoyment of the cruel and hateful ruler of the small Southern Pride.

Her mother. The Sharp Claw Pride Nari.

Vicious and crazed, the she-Tiger was feared by everyone in her Pride. After having killed her latest mate---one of Kylie's several stepfathers, in hand to hand combat---Corinne Connelly had tried to do the same thing to her own daughter.

That was the darkest secret of her past. Shivers ran down Kylie's spine, and she ran her hand over the slight scar she still bore behind her left ear. A perpetual reminder of where she had come from. A story that had been told to Hunter and no other person in the Maverick Pride.

Especially not *him*.

Her inner Tiger chuffed as thoughts of the Pride Healer filled her mind. He was the only male who had ever made her truly hurt for wanting.

Michael Turner had dark hair and eyes, like molten chocolate and he was just as seductive as her favorite treat. Everyone called him Mikey, but for some reason, she didn't like using his nickname. It made him seem flippant and youthful, bound to error, which he was not.

From what she knew of the doctor, he was well-educated and had a great love for his Pride. That sense of loyalty and honor that was innate in him attracted her every bit as much as his heavily muscled, bronze-skinned body and that Adonis face of his. Both lifted him to the level of unreachable.

He was a bona fide sex-god if the rumors were true. Not that she listened. Her she-Tiger had wanted to scratch the eyes out of the last woman she'd caught staring at him. Not that she could blame the younger she-Tigers in the Pride. After all, he looked like something out of a fantasy novel. She supposed he was really.

A gorgeous specimen of man and beast. Even his Tiger was huge and handsome. She'd noticed that on the last Pride run. Where the others wanted to show off and preen in front of the females, Michael's Tiger had stayed dutifully and steadily behind. He'd been guarding the Pride from the back and made sure none of the younger ones strayed too far.

Always courteous and kind, she'd heard his patients praise him. They flocked to the newly renovated Pride clinic that had been funded solely by the Neta and Maverick Development. The small office was attached to a much larger Colonial-style house where he lived.

It was located on Pride lands in a lot just a half mile down the road from the main house. He'd lived there as a cub with his grandmother, the old Pride Healer. Of course, this was all secondhand knowledge. She hadn't dared ask him anything about himself.

If Michael was her absolute ideal man now, then speaking to him would ruin her for life. How could she be ready to leave in an instant if she got her head turned by that dangerously sexy Tiger?

She always scoffed when he was referred to as Mikey, or even little Mikey, like he was some harmless kid. The Shifter was anything but. He was a dangerous predator hiding behind that smart and funny façade. Yes, he was kind and patient, but he was also fierce and wise with a heart of gold and a spine of steel.

Michael Turner was too good to be true. Certainly too good for the likes of her. That was why Kylie had to stay away from him. It was, for both their sakes.

She knew better than to let herself get caught in the webs that were hope, dreams, and possibilities. Michael Turner was the answer to every fervently whispered prayer and secret fantasy she had ever had, but there was no way on God's green earth she was telling him.

No way. Kylie knew predators. Once he had her

in his grasp, that man would hold on like a dog with a bone. But she refused to be a possession.

There was only one way she could remain quietly in Maverick Point, and off her old Pride's radar, and that was to live alone. She needed to keep her head down, work hard, and ignore everything else. Her younger self would have understood that.

This Kylie had perhaps grown a little too comfortable, complacent even. As a young woman she had survived by the skin of her teeth. Having crawled out of her mother's fight pit, broken and bloody, young Kylie had run as fast as she could to her beat up, old hatchback. It was not luck that had her starting the engine and zooming out of there.

Oh no, she never had any of that.

Kylie had gotten into the habit of leaving a spare set of keys under the front tire flap.

Thank fuck.

She had grabbed them with her bloodied left hand since her right one had been useless at the time. It had been broken and mangled by her mother's jaws during their gory battle.

It was good to remember, she told herself. In fact, she should never forget the danger that quite possibly still hunted her.

Kylie closed her eyes as the memories threatened

to overwhelm her. She'd been so young, so scared, but no one had stopped it or intervened. They hadn't dared to, and she'd locked herself inside her car, hoping to catch her breath before taking off.

But no luck Kylie had been given no reprieve. She'd barely closed her eyes when she'd heard her mother's roar. That cry had been deliberate. It had signaled to her Queen's Guard to hunt and kill her only daughter.

So, she did what she had to. Kylie had sucked in a painful breath and started the engine. She'd burnt rubber to get out of those South Carolina woods, driving far, far away from the old plantation home where she'd been born. Making it thus far, and Kylie had never looked back.

Three years had passed since that fateful night. Sometimes, she woke up in a cold sweat thinking her mother's Guard had found her, but then, after she'd realized she was safe, she'd relax.

She was no longer alone. Kylie was part of the Maverick Pride now, and as such, she had nothing to fear. As long as she *never ever* let her guard down.

And she wouldn't. Not for him. Not for anyone.

Kylie would never be caught unaware again.

Her phone rang, and she looked down to see a

text from Gretchen. Frowning, she read it before a smile broke out across her face.

By the way, our Nari insists we do a little karaoke for her party, so don't give me any of your shy shit. Your song has been chosen!

"Crazy heifers," Kylie muttered, shaking her head, but she was giggling all the same.

Life was good in Maverick Point. She only hoped it would last.

Chapter Three

"Mikey!" someone called his nickname from around the Pride House.

He could not see the person since the huge party tent that he and the others had just finished putting up in the massive back yard, was blocking the way.

The thing looked pretty damn good, if he did say so himself. The company they'd rented it from was run by some Lion Shifters over in Blue Valley, a neighboring town where the Blue Valley Pride was located.

Typically, he stayed away from those hair-crazed felines, but they'd needed a tent. The other men were working on moving several large tables inside, along with chairs, but he had just finished draping white cloths over the tables. The head table had needed two, which he supposed made sense since that was where the happy couple were to be seated during the shower.

"Mikey!" the female yelled again.

Sounded like Jess, he thought, wondering why the Beta's mate was yelling her head off for him.

Pierce was busy hooking up a generator to run the portable air conditions, fans, and lights, all of which were necessary due to the heat. July in New Jersey was hotter than Hades, and the Nari had made it quite clear she wanted to be nowhere without a little AC.

Not that he blamed her. Sometimes the temperature soared to triple digits, and more often than not humidity followed. Oh yeah, Pierce could surely take his time and do his thing. The AC would be greatly appreciated. Especially by their very pregnant Alpha fem.

It was some set up, he mused, grabbing a water bottle. A far cry from the tiny get together he'd envisioned when the ladies of the Pride had approached him to help. And he had the aching back to prove it.

"Mikey? Are you ignoring me?"

"Not at all, Jess. What's up?" he asked, frowning at Jessica's use of his childhood nickname.

He was still respectful and friendly in his response. She was mated to the Pride Beta, a big ass Black Bear Shifter that no one fucked with. Not that he was afraid of Brayden, he simply preferred his nose right where it was. His Tiger snorted at the insinuation that he'd be so easy a target, but Michael hushed his inner beast.

There was no sense baiting the bear. Literally or figuratively.

He turned and smiled at Jess and waited for her response. No matter what he did, he couldn't get her to stop calling him by his old nickname. Might as well stop trying, though it pained him.

Grrr.

He was the official Pride Healer now and had even finished his residency. The plaque on his door sported a real *MD* after his name too---and his name was Michael Turner. Mikey was a cub's name, and he had not been a cub for years.

"Mikey! There you are," she said at last, using the hated moniker again.

Jess stood there breathless and glowing. She looked happy, he supposed, and he was glad for her, truly. Glad, and maybe a little green with jealousy. Not because he wanted her, but because he wanted his own mate.

Ugh. Whatever.

"Aww, Mikey, why the frown?"

His Tiger chuffed at the lack of respect his Neta's sister showed him, but as always, he kept his cool. He was raised to be polite, especially when talking with one of the Pride's few and very cherished females.

"No frown. What do you need?"

"Will you help me hang up the banner we made?"

"Of course," he said, and followed her across to the other side.

He didn't see a banner in her hands, but assumed it was in the tent somewhere. This party was sure to be the Pride event of the year at the rate things were progressing. How they had escalated from a small brunch to this, he had no idea. He just hoped they had enough food. A problem that could quickly end in bloody fisticuffs for Shifters.

There were seats enough for more than double the invited guests, and he imagined more would show up. Shifter parties, especially within the Pride, had a habit of growing on the spot.

The rest of the extras would probably just lounge outside the tent, likely on or near the Adirondack chairs surrounding one of the firepits that were set up in the Pride House's massive year. That was how most of the Pride get togethers went.

Their numbers were small compared to the Wolf Shifters, but Tigers loved their get-togethers, and their space in equal measure. Food, music, laughter, and reconnecting with his Pride mates would be good.

Michael had been burying himself in work lately, ministering to the needs of the community. He was grateful for the distraction. Humming to himself as he went about seeing what Jess needed, he almost missed a step as the scent of wildflowers invaded his nostrils.

Damn it, why hadn't he prepared himself for the possibility of running into *her*?

Too late now. She was there, the one female guaranteed to make him lose his mind. The she-Cat was determined to torture him but what could he do?

He was not a pushy guy, and if she did not recognize him as hers, then maybe he was wrong.

Grrr.

His Tiger nearly flipped out at the mere suggestion of such a thing. The great striped beast pushed against his skin, begging to be set free. There was no doubt about it in his animal's mind. Kylie McNaughton was his.

Shit.

He closed his eyes and grabbed his beast by the ruff, pushing him down and taking full charge of his person. It was not an easy feat, but he managed.

"Are you alright?" Jessica asked.

"Of course," he replied.

Michael sucked in a fortifying breath, determined not to do anything untoward---like grab the vexing female, bend her over the closest table, and take what he knew in his heart of hearts was his. Maybe she would be more amenable to what the universe was clearly telling him after he made her come a time or ten.

Fuck.

He really should stop thinking about Kylie coming if he was going to be in a room full of Shifters who could undoubtedly scent his arousal.

Growling, he ran a hand over his face. Michael had an image of respectability to maintain as the Pride Healer, but all thoughts of pretense went out the window when his eyes found Kylie. He should have been prepared for the way his body reacted the second he caught sight of the beautiful female.

Predictable, he thought.

Mine, his Tiger insisted.

Michael's muscles tensed. His heart pounded. Beads of sweat formed on his brow. Even his mouth went dry.

Of all the members of the Pride, the golden-haired beauty was his own particular weakness. His animal stared out from his eyes, focusing on his quarry like the single-minded predator he was.

Not that he wanted to hurt her. On the contrary, Michael wanted to give Kylie nothing but pleasure. All of his love and devotion were hers. She owned his heart, and that was putting it mildly.

Kylie was his fated mate. He'd known it for some time now. He'd felt the truth of that statement down to his marrow, but the sweet, sumptuous female still refused to acknowledge him.

He watched her through half-closed eyelids, not really listening as Jessica prattled on with her instructions. Too aware of *her* to give the pregnant she-Cat any more than a casual ear. Michael could tell the moment Kylie realized he was there. She must have caught his scent, her nostrils flared, and her mouth formed a small o of surprise.

Her back had gone ramrod straight, but she did not turn around. Just kept right on ignoring him, as if he were nothing to her.

The thought stung, but he was a patient man. If it was time she needed, he would give it to her. What else could he do?

She stood on a ladder with one half of a banner that read "Congratulations to the Proud Parents" in her hands. The "o" in the word proud was a Tiger's paw.

Cute.

From where he stood, it looked like she was trying to thread a piece of glittery twine that someone had put through one of the tent's ceiling poles through the grommet in order to hang it. Only, she couldn't reach.

"Let me," Michael said, a plan forming in his brain.

He moved right behind her, stepping on the rung just below the one where her feet rested on the ladder.

"Ooh, um, maybe I should get down first," she said, but it was too late.

He had her good and pinned. And was already reaching for the twine.

"Nah. The ladder can hold us both," he replied easily.

"Really?" she muttered, and he could practically hear her hissing.

Ha! Good. Mad was better than indifferent. He leaned over, more than necessary, enjoying the feel of her curvaceous ass pressed against his front.

"Jess aren't you in charge of the signs? I'll just go---"

"Actually, Kylie, I was gonna make sure the karaoke machine was working okay. Did you wanna test it out with me?"

The redheaded traitor grinned and held up one of the songbooks that went with the horrible torture device.

"No!" Kylie replied, shaking her head, and almost sending the two of them toppling to the ground.

"Steady," Michael whispered in her ear, staying them both.

Her body trembled slightly against his, and fuck, his dick got hard immediately. There was no way to hide it, and honestly, he did not want to. He reveled in the sensations she caused.

Okay, so he was behaving like a dog. He would apologize.

Later.

Maybe.

Fuck.

Truth was, Michael was desperate. Catching her unawares on a ladder seemed like a good idea. After all, she was always dodging him. Running away whenever he got near her. How else was a man supposed to get near the woman he coveted?

Fine. So, it was not a good look for a majestic Tiger, but he was running out of options. She wouldn't give him the time of day. But maybe if he got her used to him---Kylie sucked in a breath, holding it, and Michael frowned. The Healer in him concerned for her well-being.

Fuck.

He didn't want her passing out. He leaned a bit more on the pretense of tying the twine, touching her waist in the process, and she gasped. The tiny shudder that ran through her body accompanied by her heightened pulse told him all he needed to know about her true feelings, and if that wasn't enough, the scent of her body's arousal would've done the trick.

Kylie wanted him.

The awareness made him practically explode with need. She couldn't hide it, but she refused to acknowledge it!

The little minx vexed him to no end. How was he going to get her to talk to him about it? Every single time he'd approached her in the past, she ran. The woman simply refused to let him get a word in.

It was as if she was afraid to be alone with him. But why? He had never done anything untoward, and he sure as heck was one of the more polite Shifters he knew. Plenty were rounders, since Shifters had large appetites in all things, sex included. But not Michael.

Fucking hell. It was all he could do not to just pick her up and throw her over his shoulder, take her to the nearest bed, and love her until she was too weak to stand.

Good plan, his beast grunted.

Shut up, he told his furry side.

Michael had to concentrate on the task at hand otherwise risk tipping them both off the ladder. His mind was still whirling even as his beast pushed him to press closer to her curvy little bottom. It took all his strength not to.

He wasn't about to dry hump the woman, but hey---he'd take what he could get.

Seeing her up on that ladder all cute and curvy---a feast for his eyes---was tempting enough. When he saw his opportunity to get close, he took it. It would just have to suffice.

For now.

Things were bound to come to a head sooner than later. Michael was still hoping Kylie would come to accept him as her fated mate on her own---maybe even be a little happy about it. Men had egos too, whatever the world might think.

Not that Michael thought of himself as particularly egocentric, but he wanted his mate to be happy to have found him. He wanted her to desire him---maybe even love him.

Perhaps not the way he loved her. Not yet anyway, but he was willing to settle for a crumb of affection at this point.

Pathetic, groaned his Tiger.

What-fucking-ever.

He took the banner from her hand and relished the way her breath caught at the seemingly platonic touch. She was not indifferent to him, despite everything she would like him to believe.

Steeling himself against any acts of stupidity, he looped the twine through the grommet, noting the subtle increase to her breathing, and the delicious scent of her growing arousal. His awareness of her was heightened and desire flared to life between the two of them.

Jess had walked away, something else having caught the she-Tiger's eye, and he was grateful. Michael did not want anyone else to have the pleasure of scenting the intoxicating floral sweetness that was Kylie's desire.

She wants me too. It's mutual, he realized, and that was really fucking good to know.

Thank fuck.

His Tiger chuffed and growled, he pushed one word at Michael. Always the same one when it came to Kylie.

Mine.

Chapter Four

Michael closed his eyes, taking a moment to savor his proximity to Kylie before he stepped back down.

She rushed down the ladder immediately after him as if she was running from a fire with her head tucked and shoulders slightly hunched in.

Everything about her physical reaction was screaming at him to get away, but he just couldn't do it. He took the ladder from her hands as she attempted to close it and moved it over to the other side of the banner.

"You got this then?" she asked, and he closed his eyes while a spike of lust surged through him at the dulcet tone.

"If you can stay and tell me when it is even, it might go a little faster," he suggested.

He saw the minute she realized Jessica had left them to it.

"Fine, but you better move like green grass through a goose. I've got better things to do," Kylie replied, her Southern accent flaring to life as she grumbled at him.

Fuck---her sass was so damn sexy.

He hid the stupid grin he knew he was wearing across his face. Must look like a simpering idiot. But how could he help himself?

She was too fucking adorable for him to not smile. The woman was driving him bonkers.

"Thanks. I can be quick, that is if that's what you want. Quick but focused So I can do the job, but *only* when you want me to be. Otherwise, I prefer to take my time," he replied with a wink.

Her eyes widened, and he guessed she understood the innuendo. That time he couldn't possibly hide his smile. He was getting to her. That was good.

New plan, wear down her defenses then when she least expects it, pounce!

Fuck. That plan was likely to get his throat torn out. Kylie was a she-Cat, not some weakling. She-Tigers were notoriously quick to react when uninvited males entered their space or territory without permission.

Michael wanted her permission. Fuck---he even dreamed about it.

Jessica and Gretchen returned to the party tent. The two women were busy adding flowers, frills, and glitter to the dozens of large round tables the men had finally finished setting up.

Gretchen was currently scolding Lance, a younger Tiger and one of the Neta's Guard, for knocking down a centerpiece. Reg, her mate, stood close by and glared at the younger man as if daring him to argue.

Jessica was shooting off rapid fire instructions at the rest of them, while casting glances at the entry-way, probably looking for her own mate.

It seemed like everyone was finding a mate within the Pride, and that was a good thing. The upcoming birth of the Neta's and Nari's cub was a meaningful event shared by all. But none of it mattered as much as Kylie did to him.

The rest of them could have all been a million miles away for all the attention Michael paid them. There was only Kylie as far as he was concerned.

Hell--- a thousand women could prance around

him butt naked, and he wouldn't see a single one of them. Not one.

No one else could compare to his pretty little kitten as far as he, and his Tiger were concerned. She was it for him. He wanted no one else.

No other female would do.

If only she wouldn't keep herself so closed off from him! Kylie was a total mystery. He hardly knew anything about her past and her background. Not that it mattered.

He still wanted her---no, he needed her, like he needed air to breathe. She was a necessity. In fact, he looked forward to finding out every one of those secrets she kept so awfully close to her.

Michael was determined to discover the many enigmas that made Kylie who she was. He was greedy for the tiniest morsel of information. No detail was too miniscule or unimportant.

What kind of music did she listen to? What kind of books did she read? He knew she liked them, because he saw her cuddled up with an old e-reader time and again.

In fact, he'd sent her a new charger after he'd heard her lamenting her old temperamental one to the Nari and the other females. That had been a memorable encounter.

The confounded woman had thrown the gift at him and demanded to know what he wanted in return. When his answer was nothing, she'd lost all steam. He'd left it on her doormat later that day with a note saying, *"I just thought you could use this and for the record, as a rule, gifts given by me do not require anything in return."*

He hoped she'd kept it, but he did not really know since she hadn't mentioned it again. But Michael still considered it a win. Hunting for the tiniest tidbit of info on her had become his most earnest hobby.

What was her favorite food? Did she like warm weather or cold better? Favorite vacation spot?

He'd take anything at this point. Wondering about her was taking up ninety percent of his waking hours. Then there was nighttime.

Fuck---it was so much worse at night. That was when images of her popped up inside his head just to torture him. All that smooth, pale skin, those glossy pink lips, her soft blonde curls, and his favorite, those celery green eyes of hers. Kylie's visage haunted him all through the long hours of the day, and at night, in his dreams. But at least there, he could touch her, talk to her, be with her.

Grrrr.

This had to stop. He needed to make her listen but was reticent to push the point. Perhaps the worst guessing game he played was the one where he tortured himself with thoughts on what she might like in bed.

It drove him mad with need almost every single night. He'd taken to shifting and stalking past her apartment when it got too bad. It was the only way to sate his animal.

After hours of watching, and listening, for any sign of her, he'd go home. Usually, by then, it was nearer to dawn. But that was the only way he'd finally succumb to sleep.

Shit.

He sounded batshit crazy, and he knew it. Running a hand over his face, he decided enough was enough.

"Kylie, I need to talk to you," he said.

"It's straight," she answered, and was already walking away towards Jessica. Damn it.

"Kylie!"

"Sorry. Busy."

She gestured in front of her but didn't turn around. He gripped the handle of the ladder, crushing the metal beneath his palms. He'd just have to content himself with watching her walk away. Not like that was any hardship.

The flowy little top she wore over curve-hugging jeans was making his own denim pants uncomfortably tight. Her hair had grown out since she'd gotten to Maverick Point. He noted the blonde curls that trailed down her back in a sweet ponytail that highlighted her youthful complexion. Michael wondered if those curls were as soft as they looked. Hell, he even pictured them spread out across his pillow like a bolt of gold satin.

The image made his cock harden, and he realized he'd be walking around bent in half if this didn't stop. He liked the platinum streaks she'd recently added, and the sole pink one beneath the crown on her head. She probably didn't know he'd noticed that little bit of wildness about her. But he did. He noticed everything.

She was, in a word, lovely with her plentiful curves and Southern sass.

"Yo, Mike. The Neta wants us."

Brayden ducked his head inside the tent and called him away before he could follow her.

His Tiger growled, but he quieted the beast. He would simply have to bide his time. Sooner or later, he told his animal, she would be his. There was no way he was giving up on her.

He followed the lumbering Bear of a man into the main house and waited for him to turn around to tell him what he wanted. The Nari had been napping when he'd gone to help with the tent, so he was not worried on that front. If it were a medical emergency, he was sure the Black Bear Shifter would have said so.

"The Neta has called a meeting," Brayden grunted as he led the way to Hunter's office.

Inside, Hunter, Reg, Lance, and Pierce were already waiting. As was someone else. An older man with a thick white beard and matching hair was sitting down, sipping on his ever present mug of tea.

Michael recognized the man well. Surprised to see him there, Michael blinked before greeting the infamous founder of *Uncle Uzzi's Magical Matchmaking Service*.

"Uncle Uzzi! Nice to see you again. What brings you to Maverick Point?" he said and shook his hand.

"Hello, Mr. Turner. I'm here to discuss something that I think you in particular might find rather interesting."

"Is that so?" he asked and looked to his Neta for guidance.

Hunter nodded. His lips were in a tight, straight line, making it clear the old Witch was there about something serious. Shifters knew how to read the room. Body language, scents, micro-expressions---they all told a story. Uncle Uzzi had brought news with him, and from the looks of it, it was bad.

"Tell me, Mr. Turner, have you told that sweet little she-Cat she's your mate yet?" he asked, blue eyes twinkling.

Michael scented ozone briefly, and he thought maybe that was the old witch's magic at work. Either way he refused to show how anxious his inner beast had grown at the mere mention of that particular subject.

"Excuse me?" he asked, taken by surprise.

"Don't play games. I am talking about Kylie McNaughton, of course. I know that you know she is your fated mate. My question is, have you told her? Have you done anything to woo her?"

Coupled with a matching glare, Uncle Uzzi's no nonsense voice had Mikey ready to spill his guts.

"Uh, Neta?" he asked and looked to Hunter for help.

This was a private matter. His Pride mates all averted their eyes, but they were still in the room. Michael was stuck, and he had no idea what to say.

"It's really better to just answer his questions," Hunter returned.

"Well, uh, Uncle Uzzi, I have not had the opportunity yet---"

"Imbecile," he grumbled and paced the room.

The old Witch waved his hand and a large fan appeared, hovering midair it began to flap as the Witch muttered and paced. Finally, Uzzi turned to face Michael with his hands in front of him.

He was looking at the younger Tiger with a scathing expression, taking him in from his head to his toes with a sneer that made the Pride Healer feel all of two feet tall. This was worse than being caught by his grandmother after a night of drinking and being stupid down by the lake when he was in college.

"Well, your limbs seem to all be intact, and Hunter assures me yo have quite a good head on those large shoulders. So tell me, Healer, what the hell are you waiting for?"

"Well, Uncle Uzzi, it's complicated---"

"Excuses."

Michael ran a hand over his head and face.

Shit.

He was an asshole, and Uzzi was right. What the fuck was he waiting for?

"The truth is, I just don't know what to say to her. I mean, I am trying not to rush her, to be patient---"

"That's hardly an answer," Uzzi snorted.

"Fine, then how about this? I am waiting for her to give me a sign---*any sign*---I need to know that she is *ready* and *willing* to be my mate. I won't pressure her, and I won't use sex to make her submit to me."

"Really? I thought you growly types simply take what you want," the Witch remarked, narrowing his furry white eyebrows. "I can see that as a Healer you were taught the benefits of waiting. That's good."

The old man sat back grinning up at the very confused Tiger. Uncle Uzzi had managed to surprise Michael with his perfectly neutral tone and almost complimentary response.

What the heck is going on?

"Uh, thank you?" Michael replied, but it sounded more like a question.

Uncle Uzzi's smile dropped as quickly as it had appeared.

This, Michael thought, *was it.*

"Young man, I appreciate what you are trying to accomplish with Kylie by waiting, but I am afraid you are out of time."

Uncle Uzzi's eyes seemed to look through him for a moment, then it was as if he were staring at nothing at all. A faint blue glow emanated from the shorter, elderly Witch, but was gone before Michael could blink.

"Tell me, what do you know about her? I mean really know," Uncle Uzzi specified.

"About Kylie?" Michael looked around the room, at the familiar faces surrounding him.

Normally, he would not discuss his female in company, but this was his Pride. Tigers who made up the Honor Guard he belonged to, and their own unimpeachable Neta. They were his oldest and dearest friends, his family.

Michael trusted them with his life, and they with his. He would trust them to keep any mate of his safe, as he would do for them. With an honest and open heart, he began to tell the old matchmaker what he knew of the sweet yet feisty Southern she-Tiger.

"I know she is beautiful, smart, clever, ambitious, talented, and kind. Sadness shines in her eyes when she thinks no one is looking, and she is a loyal friend who would risk her life to save those she loves," he recalled, and his beast growled, angry at the fact she put herself in harm's way. Michael looked around the room, making sure each male understood where he was coming from as he continued to bare his soul.

"My Tiger recognized Kylie McNaughton the moment I first laid eyes on her. You ask what I know of her, Uncle Uzzi, and this is what I know---I want her more than I have ever wanted anyone or anything in my entire life. Kylie McNaughton is the only woman in the universe for me. The she-Cat is my fated mate, and I would die for her without question," Michael finished, feeling lighter now that he had finally voiced the truth aloud after so many months of keeping it a secret.

"I see," Uncle Uzzi said, staring at the Tiger with an indiscernible look on his weathered face. "So, you know nothing about her at all!"

The old Witch shook his head and slapped his hand on the arm of the sofa.

"What are yo---"

"Oh shush," Uzzi said, hushing him while he turned to stare at the far wall.

He appeared to be in deep conversation with someone or something only he could see, and he appeared to be speaking German, if Michael was not mistaken.

"Uncle Uzzi?" Hunter waited for the old man to

finish speaking to whatever he was talking to, then the huge, bald Tiger nodded before looking toward his Beta. "Ask her to come inside."

Brayden left the room to do as his Neta asked, meanwhile, Michael's Tiger was growling inside of his mind's eye. Something was going on, and as usual, he was clueless.

Eyebrows raised, he looked about the room for any sign of what was happening, but Uncle Uzzi remained impassive. Hunter had his poker face on, and no one else seemed to be in the know. Whatever was happening, he didn't like it.

"Will someone please explain---"

"Oh, now you're impatient?" Uncle Uzzi scoffed. "Michael Turner, you have had months to talk to this woman, to get her to accept your claim, but you, sir, *dallied*. Now, I think you can wait a few moments longer."

Shit.

The old Witch was right. Michael held on to his beast, the Tiger was pacing in agitation in that metaphysical plane where he waited to be called by his human half. He listened to the sounds of footfalls in the hallway, and knew Brayden was back, and yes, he had someone with him.

Someone with delicate light footsteps. Someone

who approached cautiously. His beast surged forward. The Tiger anxious at the idea his mate was reticent about entering the room.

Of course, he could not blame her. Fearsome she-Cat she might be, but Hunter's office was chick full of hulking males and one powerful matchmaking Witch. He growled softly, and the others in the room averted their gazes. Not Hunter, of course, he just smirked. Uncle Uzzi rolled his eyes, muttering something about cats needing better training.

Whatever.

Michael just wanted Kylie to feel safe. Of course, growling even louder when the door opened was probably not the right move to inspire feelings of safety and protection.

I'm a fucking idiot.

He quieted his animal and rolled his head on his neck, loosening the tension in hopes of appearing calm. Kylie looked frightened as she entered the Neta's office. Her celery green eyes darted around the room, landing on his for a beat longer than everyone else's. But she didn't stare long.

Still, it made his beast happy. Her instinct had been to look to him, and that was one helluva feeling, he had to admit. Kylie swallowed, and eventually, her gaze found Hunter's, before she averted her eyes out of respect for the male's natural dominance. Michael sniffed the air.

Fuck.

He could scent her scrambling emotions, and they were not good. It was not what he wanted her to feel---*not at all*---especially around him. Kylie wasn't just nervous. She was outright scared. And that made him mad as hell.

"Kylie?" he asked, and as usual, she didn't respond.

That was it. The otherwise patient and rational man, who was not only a doctor but the *official* Pride Healer, lost his carefully constructed cool in his Neta's office. He felt his claws pop out one at a time, causing a few of the others to step back, regarding him warily. Michael's entire body shook until finally he opened his mouth and roared---*loudly*.

"Will someone tell me what the fuck is going on?" he snarled.

Chapter Five

Oh no.

Kylie's she-Tiger had grown very still when the Pride Beta came to find her. Brayden had smiled, trying to appear smaller and gentle, which for the enormous Black Bear Shifter, was fucking impossible.

He did not want to frighten her, and she appreciated that, but it was no use. Kylie was afraid, but it had nothing to do with Brayden.

They found me. I have to leave.

It was the only thing that made any sense. Kylie looked around the room, taking a panicked gulp of air. She almost choked on it. Closing her eyes, she tried to slow down her breathing.

Leaving town held no appeal, not at all, but what

else could she do? Kylie was never going back there, no matter what bullshit they pulled.

"Kylie?" Michael asked, and the sound of his voice caused her heart to constrict.

Still trying to calm down, she didn't reply. Kylie just couldn't. She was not strong enough to deal with whatever it was between them. Her foolish attraction to the gorgeous male had been a thorn in her side for months now, but luckily, she had resisted the urge to jump his bones.

You call that lucky?

Her she-Cat grunted her disagreement. The animal was pissed beyond reason that she had refused to acknowledge exactly what the male was to her.

And just what is that?

Kylie asked her beast angrily, but she already knew, and the knowledge broke her heart.

Mate.

"Will someone tell me what the fuck is going on?"

Michael roared the question, and she felt his anguish cutting her like a knife. His voice was filled with so much force, she trembled, but not in fear.

Her eyes snapped open, and she found him instantly, already naturally attuned to him. He was the one man she never wanted to witness her humiliation, but of course, as part of the Honor Guard, he was standing amongst them.

The Neta chuffed, using his Alpha powers to calm the angry Healer. But why should he even care? He wanted her, she knew that, but sex had nothing to do with the pure rage on his face.

There it was the true predator behind the Healer's mask. Michael Turner practically vibrated with anger and anxiety had her inner Cat demanding she go to him, but she remained rooted to the spot. Kylie's heart pounded as she looked from Hunter to the Healer, and back again.

He can't be here. Not now.

But all her silent pleading wouldn't make him disappear. Michael Turner looked around the room for an answer to his bellowed question. His body shook with anger and outrage, and it was all her fault.

Shit.

Kylie was so not prepared for this. Her stomach flipped and her pulse raced. Whatever anxiety she felt dwindled in the face of her raging arousal for this male. Dammit, she could not control herself she realized with a start.

Her nipples hardened, stomach tightened, and her sex grew hot and wet at the picture he made.

The usually staid male exuded power and emotion. He was more than just your average larger than life dominant male Shifter. Michael was educated and refined. A doctor, who had the honor of being the Pride's Healer, who was trusted and liked by all.

He was a good friend, not that she took time to get to know him personally. But Kylie had heard the females speaking highly of him, and she had to learn to ignore the ones who often drooled over the ridiculously hot man.

Michael was gorgeous. He had the same muscular physique most Shifters had, but unique to him was his ability to put anyone and everyone at ease in his presence. Not typical for such a powerful Tiger to accomplish. But necessary. She imagined he would find it difficult to care for people if they were scared shitless in his presence.

Still, good traits aside, Kylie had carefully avoided him. She'd expected he was a little full of himself what with his proper education and all. Especially when compared to her back country home-schooled learning.

She was not stupid, but she couldn't help but worry about how he would take her lack of formal education. Would he sneer or make fun? Many had.

No, her she-Tiger insisted.

Mate.

Kylie ignored her beast. She could never take a mate. That would require too much of her. She could not let her guard down. Not ever.

Whatever this was, whatever was happening now, this conversation was not for his ears. Kylie frowned, an angry hiss slipped out of her mouth. She wanted to run away and scream at the injustice of it all, but she stayed put. Rooted to the spot.

What would he think after he heard her story? Would he still look at her with those smoldering dark eyes if he knew her own mother wanted her dead?

Would he think her a little nothing of a person if she told him the only learning she had was at the hands of her dead father who'd taught her to read and basic mathematics?

What would he say if she told him her mother had killed her father, the only person who ever cared about Kylie, who gave her books, and little else, because it was all he had to give?

She shuddered at the thought of seeing even the smallest fraction of revulsion in those decadent dark eyes of his. Kylie refused to be cowed down and made to feel ashamed of her past. It was not like she could help it.

Kylie had tried to overcome her upbringing. She had taught herself everything she knew about sewing out of necessity when she was just a kid. A growing girl with no money for clothes, she did what she had to in order to keep herself covered.

Do not look ashamed, her Tiger told her. *Look how far you've come.*

She knew she should be proud of her success with *Kisses By Kylie* and her upcoming *Mommies By Kylie*. She had turned into a shrewd businesswoman, and could now boast a steady stream of income, which was more money than anyone in her entire former Pride could claim.

Still, there was that tiny fear that she wasn't good enough. And that truly sucked.

Michael Turner.

She closed her eyes against his questioning gaze. He was the one man she couldn't seem to get out of her head no matter what she did, and now, he would have a front row seat to witness all her past humiliations.

On the bright side, she wouldn't have to wonder how he felt anymore. It would be painfully obvious once her secrets were exposed, and wish as she might, Kylie was powerless to stop it. She took one more moment to admire his physical perfection.

Michael was taller than her by more than a foot, and twice as wide. He was positively enormous, even for a Tiger Shifter. The rippling muscles of his arms and pecs gave way to washboard abs and powerful legs.

She had always loved a man with strong thighs, and if she were being honest, Michael's were thicker than any rugby player's she ever saw.

Yummmm.

Kylie knew she was cute, even though she was plenty plump. She'd never been tall. In fact, she was downright tiny when it came to height. Of course, her ample hips, large breasts, and soft belly made up for what she lacked in height. She had clear skin and bright eyes, full lips too. But none of that could make up for her past.

Her cheeks burned with embarrassment as she stood, front and center, in the closed in office. The energy in the room seemed to be all over the place in terms of emotion. Mostly, she felt his questioning glare and rising anger.

If only she could find the nerve to answer him. At the moment, her she-Tiger was pushing against her skin. The she-Cat wanted closer to the tall, sexy as sin man.

Mate, her inner she-Tiger growled softly.

The beast inside of her recognized him as her one and only fated mate, but Kylie couldn't go there. She could *never* go there.

"They know where I am?" she addressed Hunter, ignoring the pleading look on Michael's handsome face.

"Yes."

"I see. How long do I have?"

"Dear, I think you should sit down, and explain to everyone the circumstances that brought you here."

She turned to Uncle Uzzi, listening to his clearly spoken words, but not really hearing him. Kylie looked at the elderly Witch, whose piercing blue eyes seemed to see right through her.

"I don't see why," she said honestly, and she didn't.

"Because, my sweet child," Uncle Uzzi began, his expression one of deep sympathy. "They deserve to know."

That seemed simple enough, she supposed. The Shifters in the room had risked a lot by taking her in. She should tell them the truth. Even if it hurt like all get out.

"Please, come and sit." Uncle Uzzi gestured to an empty chair, but Kylie made no move to sit down.

Nerves had her sucking in a deep breath before slowly exhaling. Where to start? That was always the problem, wasn't it? She supposed the beginning really was the best place.

"I grew up in a small, poor Pride in South Carolina, the *Sharp Claw Pride*," Kylie began.

She tried to remain detached but felt herself slip slowly into the past. Her gaze settled on a corner of the room where sunlight filtered through the blinds. She watched the dust motes floating in the air, not even minding when her South Carolina accent came out full force as she told her story to the room.

"Life was okay at first, if a little unorthodox. My father and mother were not married or mated in any traditional sense. You see, Daddy was too low in the hierarchy to suit the female who gave birth to me. My mother was the daughter of the Neta. She came into power, ruling the Pride as Nari when I was just a baby--- Funny, I don't ever remember her not being in charge. She ran things with an iron fist back then, I imagine she still does. Our little backwoods town, more like a holler really, had no school, no stores, and we were strongly discouraged from mixing with normals in neighboring towns. To the outside world, we looked like some religious cult or ex-hippie commune. I suppose. But that was that---"

Kylie paused and cleared her throat, remembering the early days when she didn't know about the kind of cruelty that fed her Pride.

"Summers were plenty hot, and we were so damn poor, but we had blue skies and green fields and Daddy had taught me to fish in a nearby creek. I lived with my father until he was, well, you can imagine. Anyway, there was an old wise woman in the Pride who could tell if one of us was gonna shift or not, and my mother waited. She had to determine whether I would have the gift before I was deemed worthy of her attention. How I prayed I would be a *normal*," Kylie explained, closing her eyes, her voice catching on the last word.

"Go on," coaxed Hunter when her nerves threatened to strangle her.

She looked at the Neta, then stole a glance at Michael, seeking comfort where she had no right to expect it.

Damn it, but the man seemed to know. He moved a step closer to her, and the heat from his body warmed her suddenly chilled skin. She cleared her throat again and continued.

"Her *Queen's Guard* came for me one hot afternoon. They took me to the Pride House and locked me in a small room in the cellar. My father was taken away too, but I didn't know where until much later. I was given food and water and bathroom privileges. I had no friends, and like the other few cubs of the Pride, I was not allowed to go to school. Thankfully, I had already learned to read at my father's knee, and eventually, I was given an old, battered eReader by one of the kinder males who were assigned to watch me. I had to keep it secret. Charging it by day. Reading only at night."

She smiled at the memory, a tear rolling down her face at the thought of what had happened to that kind male. Gene was his name.

"When I had my first shift, my mother came for me. She did not even say a word, simply walked me to my father's cell where she forced me to watch while she attacked him viciously. He'd been half-starved and was too weak to fend her off. She sliced his throat open with her claws, and he bled to death in front of me," she recalled, her voice a dull monotone. She betrayed no emotion, having cried too many tears to have any left now.

How many times had she relived the horrible moment when her only loving parent had been taken from her?

Too many.

Dammit, she'd been such a fool to think she'd actually gotten away.

"My mother's *Queen's Guard* took me away after I had spent Lord knows how long with my father's broken and bloodied body. They brought me to the circle where she broke her enemies. There, she had me tied to stakes driven into the dry ground and I was beaten," she continued, ignoring the sharp intake of breath that came from just about everyone in the small space.

"It wasn't long before she stopped it, rejoicing at how easy it was to break me then. I was twelve, and I was small. I knew nothing about fighting. The men took me back to my room and a new guard was placed at the door. Our Healer wasn't called until much later and by then the worst injuries had healed, but the bones were not set right. He had to re-break my hand just so I could hold a fork---"

A snarl nearby had her bringing her head up where she met a pair of familiar and fierce dark eyes. They were glowing amber with his beast.

"It's alright," she said, wanting to comfort the owner of those eyes. "After that, I was pretty much ignored for the next few years. Later, my mother formed an alliance with a nearby rogue streak and married their leader. He was kind, my stepfather. At least, he was to me. That's probably why she killed him next," she lamented.

"*Corinne Connelly*, Nari of the Sharp Claw Pride defeated him in hand to hand combat, but Jacob Pitt was harder to kill than my Daddy. His former streak, having been ingratiated into the Pride, were outraged, and came after my mother," she said.

"Corinne was a smart woman though. She knew she couldn't defeat three enormous males at once, so she offered them something better. My mother offered to form a marriage alliance with one of them. She was gonna let them pick one of their own, and that male would get to be her mate," Kylie's voice stuck as she recalled the next round of events with a shudder.

"What happened then?" Brayden, a Bear Shifter who also happened to be her friend Jessica's mate and the Pride Beta, interrupted.

"One of them laughed, and that cost him an ear," she continued, detachedly.

If Kylie could pretend those horrible things had happened to someone else, it would be easy, she figured.

"The others had a better plan. They told her since she was no longer able to bear cubs that she should offer them someone else. Someone who carried her Alpha blood but was younger."

The horror of their words still haunted her to this day. Fear and loathing made her shudder, and she was grateful when someone handed her a bottle of cold water. She looked up to say thank you but could not utter a word. Michael's face was composed, but his eyes were those of his beast.

The Tiger was barely contained, but for some reason Kylie did not fear him. Her own she-Cat rose inside, and the look that sizzled between them seemed to last for an eternity.

Chapter Six

"They wanted you," Michael said, his voice an earthy growled that sent shivers of awareness rolling through Kylie.

"Yes," she confessed, and closed her eyes on the wave of nausea that followed.

"My mother was jealous and angry at being humiliated in front of her circle. She told them they could all have their turn with me if I survived. Then, she attacked."

"Your mother attacked you?"

His voice was low, almost a whisper, but she could feel the tightly leashed fury he was holding onto inside his softly spoken words. Kylie merely nodded before continuing to tell her sad little tale.

"She broke my arm, and my jaw, mangled my

hand, dislocated my shoulder. Hell, I think she almost killed me. Somehow, I got the upper hand. I knocked the wind out of her. While her *Queen's Guard* tended her, I ran. Crawled out of the pit and made it to my car. I put it in gear, but before I peeled out of there, I heard her roar, ordering my death. I never drove so fast. But I got out of there and I have never looked back."

The silence in Hunter's office was deafening. Kylie knew the laws of Shifters were complicated, sometimes brutal, and terrible. If her old Pride wanted her back, something had to have happened. She closed her eyes, waiting for the ax to fall.

"I want to thank you, Kylie, for sharing that with us," Uncle Uzzi said, while the others in the room did their best to calm their agitated beasts.

She knew enough of the Maverick Pride to understand this story would horrify them. Their world was so much different than hers. So much prettier, safer, and kinder than where she'd been raised.

"Do you know what happened to your mother after you left?"

"No, but I assume she is after me again."

"Actually, I am *not sorry* to inform you that your mother had been killed by those same rogues she took into her Pride shortly after your escape," Uncle Uzzi stated to the sound of reverberating growls across the room.

Kylie could hardly believe it.

Her mother was dead.

"Then who is after me?"

"This might be hard to hear," Hunter said, stepping forward. "You see, Kylie, most of the Pride fled after your mother's death. The remaining streak brought in more rogues and scoundrels, outcasts of other Prides. Under the Sharp Claw Pride title, they have remained part of the Shifter Council. Now, these males have been fighting each other for control ever since. They have gone through several leaders in the last few years alone."

"This is true," confirmed Uncle Uzzi.

"You see, dear, I was contacted by someone from the inner circle of the new Sharp Claw Pride's Neta just the other day. A Tiger Shifter by the name of Waylon Pitt, Jacob's younger brother. He has control now, well, for the time being. He called me to find you, Kylie."

"Waylon?" she asked, shuddering as a fresh memory came rushing back to her.

The bearded man had been older than her by at least twenty years. He'd given off a bad vibe, or so she had thought the first time she'd laid eyes on him. He was not like his older brother, the man her mother had first chosen to mate. Waylon was nasty and cruel, always leering whenever her mother had made her sit with them during meals and runs.

The worst was the way he smelled, like a mixture of the most offensive body odor, sickly sweat, and urine. Being a Shifter, she had no idea how he could stand to be near himself. She had no respect for the foul male, and no desire to be hunted by him either.

"How close is he to finding me?"

"He gave me the name of a town where he thought you were staying. Said I should look for you at Maverick Point, and that he wanted to employ my service since he believes you are his mate."

"No! I mean, what did you tell him?"

"I told him to give me a week, and that I would get back to him."

"I have to go. I have to get my things," Kylie mumbled, trying not to panic.

Waylon thinks I am his mate. No! He just wants to use me.

"No, you can't leave!" Michael barked.

"What? What do you have to say about it?"

Kylie narrowed her eyes and turned, facing the

man she'd been doing everything in her power to avoid for months, and all for this very reason.

Michael Turner might be good to look at, but he didn't know what those men were like. No honorable Shifter could ever imagine.

They were scum. Low lives who wanted to use her, break her for their own amusement. To hold her like a prize to rule over the Pride her own mother had run into the ground.

"I have plenty to say," he growled.

"No, you don't. And I need to go," she said, and made to move around him, but he blocked her path.

"Where will you go that's safer than here?" Michael demanded.

"Don't you get it?" she yelled, crying now where she'd not shed a tear for so long. Angrily, she wiped at her face.

"I can't bring them here. You don't understand what they are. Besides, this is my problem, it has nothing to do with you," she said.

Kylie's eyes held his for the first time in---well, *ever*---and she swore sparks of electricity sizzled between them.

Her stomach clenched and beads of sweat began to form on her brow.

Oh fuck. Oh no. Not now.

Mating fever. She had heard of it, and she could not be sure, but something was hitting her and hitting her hard. Her nipples tightened painfully, her sex clenching on air.

Fuck. She could just ignore it. She had to.

Her she-Tiger growled and hissed, the beast at odds with her human half. It felt strange to fight with her inner animal. After all, she was the only one who'd ever been there for her for years.

Mate, the she-Cat insisted.

No.

She would not acknowledge her beast's mournful roar. She couldn't afford to think about that. Kylie was not meant for happily-ever-afters. The best she could do was survive.

"Kylie---"

"It's not your concern, Michael," she growled, refusing to let her body rule her mind.

She ignored the next wave of cramping. If she went into heat maybe some other male could---

No.

She already knew she could never take another to bed.

Dammit.

Why now? She wanted to scream, but she had no time for self-indulgences like that.

Waylon knew where she was. He and his men had hunted her all the way north to Maverick Point. And when they found her, well, the bastard would drag her back to South Carolina like a prize. Once there, they would fight over her like a juicy steak.

One thing she knew for sure, Kylie was never going back there. She would die first.

"Is that what you think? It's none of my business?"

"That's right," she returned.

This time Michael was the one who scoffed. She couldn't blame him. She'd treated him badly, and she knew it. But he was young, educated, good-looking. He could find someone else. Someone who could give him things she couldn't.

Like peace.

Kylie refused to bring blood and violence to his door, to any of their doors. This Pride had given her sanctuary, but now it was time to go.

"Children!" Uncle Uzzi clapped his hands to get their attention.

"Now, Kylie, there is a better way to stop the Sharp Claw from holding any claim on you. You see, Waylon is not only saying you are his mate. He is appealing to the Council saying you were stolen from them when you were underage---"

"What?! He is crazy! Besides, what better way could there be? I have to leave. Period."

"Shh, it is not your turn to talk, dear," Uncle Uzzi grunted, shaking his finger and blue sparks of magic sizzled in the air.

Kylie looked at Michael then, and they both turned to face the only Witch in the room. Uncle Uzzi was formidable, she would give him that. Seeing the older Witch wearing a wickedly satisfied smirk had chills running up Kylie's arms.

Uncle Uzzi glanced once at the Neta as if waiting for approval before he continued to address the room.

"Well, it seems my talents can come into play here after all. As you all know, I have helped some members of your Pride find their mates---"

"What are you saying?" Kylie interrupted.

"First, if you think I am going to let you---*the woman who many of my female clients' are raving about as their new favorite lingerie designer*---walk away without a trace, you are mistaken, my dear," Uzzi began, ignoring the groans and closed eyes of the men in the room.

Even big boys couldn't handle talking about a woman's underwear, Kylie thought and snorted.

Pussies.

"As I was saying," Uncle Uzzi commanded the attention of the room. "Those rogues only want you because you remain free, unmarked and unmated."

"I know," Kylie said. "They only want to mate me to better control the Pride," she said, revolted at the very idea.

"Yes," nodded Uncle Uzzi.

She had the feeling that Uncle Uzzi's unblinking sapphire-blue stare saw way more than anyone could've guessed. Way more than she wanted the older Witch to see. Kylie swallowed and waited for her to continue.

"They see you as a prize, their prize, since they are claiming you belong to them. They believe they can use you to curry favor with the remaining members of the Sharp Claw Pride as their rightful heir. The stronger Tigers have already left. They wouldn't follow a Pride with no clear leader. The remaining rogues want to use you to force the weaker ones to follow whichever of them gets their mark on you first."

"I will never go back there," she vowed.

"And they will never stop hunting you," Uzzi countered.

"I'll go---"

"No, you can't leave. We will protect you---"

Michael spoke, stepping forward, and her heart squeezed at his words.

"And they will wage a war, claiming you do not have the right to hold her as she is their Pride mate. You must admit, no formal declaration of switching Prides was given," Uncle Uzzi cited the old Shifter law to resounding growls and grunts from the Shifters in the room.

"Look, I appreciate all of you, and the Maverick Pride has been good to me. But I won't bring bloodshed here. I am not worth it---" Kylie blurted.

"What? Of course, you are," Michael said, and he sounded crushed.

"We are your Pride now, Kylie, and we are Shifters. Bloodshed is what we do," Hunter said, smiling.

"Yes, Neta, but I can't risk endangering Elissa and your cub or any of you. Not for me," she argued, trying to make them see reason.

"I will leave---"

"No," Michael shook his head.

"Before you decide that," Uncle Uzzi said with an edge in his voice and a glare at Michael. "I have another solution."

"What's that?" Kylie said, knowing the Witch meant well but it was hopeless.

Whatever they decided now, she would not endanger the Pride. No matter what. She could not allow those rogue bastards to come and start a war here.

Not for her.

She would have to leave in the dead of night to avoid detection. Her mind raced with ideas even as her heart thudded sorrowfully inside of her chest. There were precautions to take, things she'd have to do to avoid getting caught by Jess or Gretchen, or even Elissa.

"Do not think like that, Kylie. Stop it now," commanded Uncle Uzzi, and she looked up surprised to see the older Witch frowning. "I said, I have a solution, Kylie McNaughton, and it does not involve you running."

"Alright," Kylie answered unsteadily. "I'll hear it, before I make a decision."

"Good. That's all I ask."

Uncle Uzzi smiled triumphantly and looked around the room before zeroing in on Kylie once more.

"What if you were already mated by the time they get here?"

Confusion furrowed her brow, and she cocked her head to the side. Her she-Tiger pressed against her skin. The great big animal wanted more information.

"What?" she asked as she tried to make sense of Uncle Uzzi's words.

"Yes," growled Michael in response, and he seemed to grow taller as he nodded his assent. But his assent to what exactly, she wondered.

"What are you saying yes to?" she said looking from Uncle Uzzi to him, then back again. "What is he saying yes to?"

The Witch's grin grew wider, and judging from the predatorial look on Michael's face, and the ethereal blue lights swirling around Uzzi's head, she had the feeling he knew what he was agreeing to.

Oh hell no!

Kylie wanted to stomp and growl, but even doing so would not help her to reason with the man. So, she turned to Hunter.

"Neta, you have to stop him---"

"Neta," Michael said at the same time, cutting her off effectively. "I am officially announcing my intention to mark and claim Kylie McNaughton, as a true and eligible male from an honored family of the Maverick Pride, I will have *her*, and no other, as my mate from now until the end of time!"

Holy fucking shit, she gasped.

Michael Turner, Maverick Pride Healer, had invoked the *Ancient Rite of Proclamation.*

It was so fucking sexy that her whole body flushed in response, and her ferocious, and somewhat skittish she-Tiger, purred.

Loudly.

Purrrrrrrrr.

But Kylie could not just let that slide, so she turned to the big male who was practically vibrating with energy, and was, admittedly, more attractive than any other she had ever seen. Still, she slapped his face good and hard.

"You *buttlickingcatnipsniffingfureatingasshat!*"

Chapter Seven

"W hat?!"

"Mikey, are you sure?"

"Holy shizzle!"

"Damn bro!"

Michael's heart was pumping a mile a minute. Thunder roared in his ears and his Tiger snarled inside his mind's eye. He felt his fingertips burn with the need to extend his claws and his fangs begged to be set free.

"Mikey? Mike. Michael!"

He turned his head, and stared at his Neta, holding the powerful man's gaze for a beat before averting his eyes out of respect.

It was kinda sorta difficult for him to look at the male since his dick was rock hard with the need to claim his mate. Hunter focused his steely teal gaze on his Pride Healer.

"Do you understand what you've done?" Hunter asked, eyebrows raised.

"Yes, Neta," Michael replied, his voice rough with his Tiger. "I completely understand."

"Excuse me a damn minute," the feisty little she-Cat growled and stalked towards the desk, almost tripping in the process.

She pushed Michael's hand away when he would've steadied her, and fuck, that bit of temper only served to make his cock harder. Damn, but he liked a fiery woman.

Actually, he liked *this* woman. Only this woman.

It was simple as that. Everything about her called to him. It had ever since he'd first seen her, but he'd been dragging his feet the whole time. And for what?

He'd been in love with her for months. Pining for her. Waiting. Biding his time. And he almost missed it. Well, no more. He would claim her, knowing she was his and had been since the dawn of time. He believed that deep in his heart, in his very soul.

Michael *would* claim Kylie.

Now.

Tonight.

She would be his.

Finally.

Grrr.

Ever since she had viciously defended the Nari in Jessica's shop, Michael had wanted her. He had treated her for her wounds. Had the sweet and fierce she-Cat under his care for all of twenty-four hours before she'd walked out of the clinic and insisted on healing by herself in her *own damned bed* as she had put it.

Watching as she had walked out on him in the same tiny paper gown all his patients wore was the hardest day of his life. Michael had almost lost his shit entirely. It had taken all of his strength and will power not to rush after her and toss her over his shoulder caveman-like.

The wounds she'd allowed him to treat were superficial at most. A thing for which he was eternally grateful. It was the scars she'd kept hidden on her back and wrist that had worried him.

Shifters did not usually bear scars. When they did, it was at the hands of extreme abuse. Now that he knew who was behind it, hunting them down was on his *must do asap* list. Right after all the things he wanted to do to and with her.

"Look, Hunter, I don't know what Dr. Macho here thinks he is doing, but you can't mess with

Waylon and his crew. These men are no better than mindless animals. They have no boundaries at all. I'm not staying here, and endangering you all-"

"You aren't going anywhere."

"Oh, really, and why is that?" she taunted.

"Mine," growled Mikey, and he felt his Tiger rise in confirmation.

He could only imagine how he looked. Half wild with his dark eyes glowing amber in the dim light of the office.

Fuck it.

"I invoked my intent to claim, unless another comes forward, you are mine."

"Fuck you," she growled.

"Yes," he replied, smirking at her.

And crude or not, he meant every word. Kylie was staying right there with him. He heard her breath catch in her throat, and watched her own eyes dilate in surprise, and arousal.

Now, that he'd announced his intentions, there was no way in hell that she was leaving Maverick Point. Not when he was the only one in the universe who could keep her safe and sound. He took a step forward, ready to seal the deal right then and there.

"Easy there," snapped Uncle Uzzi, but he still pressed forward. "I said back off, pussycat!"

Michael's Tiger hissed at the offensive tag, but he backed off when the older, powerful Witch slapped his nose like his grandmother had back when he'd been an errant cub.

He sniffed and shook his head, taking another step back for good measure. But he didn't stray too far from Kylie. He couldn't. Being near her was a biological imperative. Especially now that he'd announced his intent.

"Enough of that or I'll have your tail for a neck-tie," Uncle Uzzi remarked and rolled his eyes. "Now, call me crazy, but it's been a damn long time since anyone has claimed the *Ancient Rite of Proclamation.* If my memory of Tiger Shifter Pride Laws serves me correctly, the female doesn't have a choice unless she is championed by a father or brother. That about right?"

"That is correct, Uncle Uzzi," said Hunter.

"Okay. Now, Kylie, do you have a living male relative?"

"No," his soon-to-be mate growled.

"I see. Anyone else who would defend you?" Uncle Uzzi continued to question her, and Michael frowned. Was the Witch looking to hurt Michael's chance at finally having her.

His inner logic told him the old Witch was

simply trying to offer her a way out. He was looking out for her, and Michael had to appreciate the effort, even as he resented it.

"I will champion her, if she refuses," Hunter offered, and Michael tensed.

He had no wish to fight his Neta, but he would. For her he would.

"No. I can't let you do that, Hunter," Kylie said, and turned to Uncle Uzzi. "Besides, I think it has to be a blood relative, and I have no one, Neta, Uncle Uzzi.," she replied, nodding at each male.

"You have me," Michael answered.

"Yes, you certainly do," snorted Uncle Uzzi. "Okay, so, here we go. Michael, do you promise to behave in an honorable and respectful fashion to your chosen mate?"

"I do," he answered.

"Great! Now Kylie," Uncle Uzzi began.

"There has to be another way, this won't stop Waylon," she insisted, turning her big celery green eyes on him.

Didn't she know Michael could not care less? He would fight the whole damn world for her if necessary. She just had to learn to trust him.

"It will, or he will have to deal with forces far more powerful and unbending than he's ever seen.

Not to mention a Pride full of angry pussies if he even thinks about messing with you, my dear," Uncle Uzzi stated.

"You don't know what you're doing, Michael." Kylie turned her big, sparkling green eyes on him. "Please, take it back."

It was the first time he'd ever heard his full name on her lips. The entire room seemed to fade away, as his Tiger surged forward. She was the only one there. The only thing that mattered.

So beautiful. Those eyes, that hair, those curves, her scent, she was perfection itself.

"Never. I will never take it back," he stated, watching his very curvy, petite little kitten as she finally realized he meant business.

She placed her hands on her wide hips, dragging his attention there. Fuck, she was perfect. His eyes travelled farther up to her narrow waist, then on to her big, heavy breasts, and up the gentle slope of her neck.

They went further still to that mouth of hers that was currently ever-so-slightly open, begging for his attention, and Michael licked his lips. His Tiger growled softly.

"Okay pussies, listen up. Michael, if you ever step one foot out of line, I will personally tear your tail off, so you won't be able to tell what's left from your asshole, got it? And Kylie dear, this may be unortho- dox, but it was always in the cards for you, you know that don't you? Good. Everyone out, Let's give the new couple a little space."

Michael only half listened to the shuffle of feet, and to Hunter's minor protest that it was his office after all. The Neta might be right, but Michael did not care. He paid little attention to the others as they emptied the room.

He simply couldn't. His senses were so completely full of her, every last ounce of his atten- tion was rooted to the spot where Kylie stood.

She was his entire reason for being. Michael could sense her waning anger and growing arousal as if it were a living tangible thing, a separate entity, taunting him with the space that existed between them.

Light and airy, her fragrance sizzled in the room, wildflowers with a hint of Tabasco sauce. His own sweet and sassy Southern belle. She'd lost most of her accent, but every now and then it slipped through, and damn near drove him wild with raging lust and need.

"Michael," she whispered, and closed her eyes

even as she faced him. "If we do this, it will be too late. You won't be able to take it back---"

"Don't you know the truth yet, Kylie?"

"What's the truth?"

She blinked her eyes and scrunched her nose in annoyance. Exhaling deeply, he knew she was annoyed, fighting her own desires, and damn it, if he was not mistaken, he would swear she was going into heat.

"Truth is, I've wanted to do this since I first saw you."

Michael moved in swiftly and placed his hands on either side of her face. Gently, he held her there, savoring the feel of her soft skin against his palms. He wanted her to look at him, and she did. Her big green eyes practically swallowed him whole, making him even harder in his pants.

Fuck, she was so pretty. Kylie gasped softly, and he was loving the increase of her pulse as he leaned down. Her breath caught in her throat even as the scent of her arousal grew thicker.

"It's been you, *mon petit chaton*. Since the very first time I saw you. It has always been you," he whispered, and finally, pressed his mouth to hers.

The spicy floral flavor that was all Kylie burst across his tongue, and he growled, nipping her lower lip with his fangs. She brought out the beast in him, and he was powerless to stop it.

On, and on, and on---lips touched, tongues twirled, and growls exchanged as Michael held her face exactly where he wanted it.

Stars and planets aligned and dispersed, whole universes died and were born, and the sun itself burnt out only to be reborn in the time it took to kiss her properly.

And it was so much better than he'd ever imagined.

Chapter Eight

Her kiss swallowed him whole, taking him from where he was standing and rocketing him into infinity. Her sweet, lush body pressed against his, and she moaned. Michael was a total goner.

Kissing Kylie was like an addiction he did not even know he had. His tongue delved into the hot cavern of her mouth, tasting every inch of her, and relishing in her flavors. He wanted to consume her, to swallow her down, to stamp himself all over her heavenly body.

Kylie was pure ambrosia. Kissing her sent him spiraling, she was his heaven on earth, his weakness, his strength, his everything, and he was never letting go.

"Mine," he growled, pulling her closer.

Kylie's arms came around his neck, and she opened her eyes. He found her she-Tiger staring out at him, ring of golden fire circled her celery green irises. His cock grew even harder.

"Need you, Kylie. Want you. Please?" he asked, and it was a question.

Fuck. He would get down on his knees and beg if she needed him to. Michael's need had reached a level of urgency he could not have anticipated just seeing her staring at him, eyes glowing with her beast. He waited, barely holding onto his own Tiger, until she nodded her head.

Thank fuck.

Without words, he lifted her in his arms and carried her out the door.

"Micha---"

"Not a word."

"But I---"

"Is your answer still yes?" he asked, pausing briefly, and looking at her intently.

"Yes."

"Good. Just let me get us out of here before I lose my head, kitten."

Eyes wide, Kylie nodded. His car was parked on

the side of the Pride House, but he made it there in seconds.

Michael loaded her carefully inside, racing around to his seat before peeling out of the driveway.

"Where are we going?" she asked with that same breathless hitch in her voice that sent shockwaves of need spiking straight through to his steel hard cock.

The woman was trying to kill him!

"Our house," he said, and felt the truth in his words.

Over the last sixth months he'd made several renovations to the home where he'd been raised with his grandmother. New floors, new paint, new furniture. Every improvement, every change made were *her* in mind. He'd even left it sort of plain and bare, hoping she would fill the space with what she liked. Nerves had him doubting his choices.

Did he think too much of himself and his chances by doing all that? Would she think so? Fuck.

His Tiger pushed all the negativity away. None of that was important. All he wanted was to make her happy, keep her safe, bring her pleasure. Making her feel good was all the beast wanted before he marled her with his mating bite.

Fuck. Yes. Mine.

They walked up the back patio stairs to the private entrance to his, no, *their* home. Kylie stalled, her breathing was short, and a little shallow, and he tried to calm himself. Michael led her down the hallway, with a steady hand on her waist.

Once inside the large living room, Kylie turned to face him. A large, floor to ceiling window faced outward overlooking a stand of pine trees, allowing sunlight to filter through and onto her beautiful blonde head.

He was glad he'd had special, one way glass installed so he could see out, but no one could peer in. This moment was his. Kylie was finally right where he wanted her, and damn did he want her. Michael was dying to touch her, to strip her bare, to see every inch of her clearly defined in the light of day.

"I feel like I should say something," Kylie began, unsure, and he could not blame her.

"I apologize about before, telling you to shush," he began, feeling his cheeks warm. "Fact is, Kylie, you can say anything you want to me. Anything at all."

"I, uh---" Kylie looked down, and he scented her embarrassment. It brightened her cheeks, strengthened her fragrance. "I've, um, never actually done this kind of thing," she admitted.

Michael grinned and stepped closer to her. He couldn't help it. She was like his moon. He was drawn to her as if by gravity or reeled in like a fish from the sea. Maybe she was more like the sun in his universe, and he was just a planet, orbiting round and round just to be near her.

He grinned and shook his head. Michael was a doctor, not a poet. But she was all those things to him and more still. He was destined to be with her. Michael believed that in his soul.

His sweet Kylie was every bit as glorious as the sun, but he wouldn't die if he touched her. Oh, he would burn alright. They both would.

But it would be a slow, deliberate kindling. A joining of bodies and souls, of their inner beasts and their human sides.

The manifestation of their consummation would be a *matebond*. An ethereal force that tied them together, bound them for life. That was what happened when fated mates found one another. Every fiber of his being screamed that one truth at him.

"What kind of thing?" he asked, intensely awaiting her reply.

"I know Shifters have different morals than normals, but, you see, I've been trying to stay alive so I never---"

She paused, and he realized he'd started growling.

"I am sorry," he said gruffly. "The thought of you being alone and in danger---"

"No," she said, stepping closer to him. "I mean, I appreciate the concern, but it led me here. And, well, what I am trying to say is I've never been intimate with anyone."

Her confession hung in the air between them, and Michael did not know how to react. If he threw his head back and roared, she would think he was a Neanderthal. If he contemplated her situation, he would lose his mind for the time she had lost in her hectic youth. He figured he should just tell her the truth about what he was thinking.

"I know this makes me an even bigger freak than you must think---"

"Hey now," he said, shaking his head. He moved closer, wrapping her in his arms, and smiled when she didn't pull away. She felt good in his arms, her curves molding to the hard planes of his large body.

Other female Shifters were thin and hard, but not his mate. She was soft and perfect, powerful, but caring, and after all she had been though, she was letting him hold her, and that was a miracle he would gladly fall down on his knees to praise god for.

"I am sorry, kitten," he murmured, kissing her nose, her cheek, her head, everywhere he could touch. And between kisses, he talked. "I am sorry that you lost that time. Time when you should have just been a kid. Time when your biggest worry should have been your prom dress, or whether to kiss your sweetheart on top of the Ferris wheel, or any number of silly kid things," he finished.

"My life did get better, after I left," she whispered, leaning into his caresses, and damn that made him feel ten feet tall.

"I'm glad it did. I'm thankful you found your way here. And if I am being honest, I can't say I am not happy you saved yourself for me," he confessed, baring his soul.

"I didn't know it at the time," she teased.

"Kylie," he growled kissing her hard and fast. "You are driving me insane, you know that don't you?"

"Am I?" she asked, wonder shining in her bright eyes.

"You are without a doubt the sexiest woman I

have ever met."

"How can I be sexy? I've never had sex. What if I disappoint---"

"Shhh. You are my mate, kitten. And what we are about to do to each other, I've never done either," he whispered before claiming her lips.

"Yes, but, oh---"

Michael tipped her backward, licking a trail from her neck to her earlobe. Fuck, she tasted like sunshine and sin. A delicious combination of everything he ever wanted, and nothing he had ever tasted.

Kylie moaned into his mouth, and he swallowed the sound, his kisses moving up her chin to her perfectly plump lips.

She shivered in his arms, and he made a note that she was sensitive just there beneath her ear. He licked the spot and nuzzled her, spreading his scent on her sublimely soft skin.

"I--- oh, do that again, please," she murmured as his hands made short work of her top and pants, grazing the hard pebbles that were her nipples through the sheer bra she had on.

"Did you design this?" he growled, as he backed her onto the couch and nuzzled her breasts with his face.

"Yes, um, do you like it?" she whispered, and he watched in amazement as she blushed and looked away from him.

"Keep your eyes on me, kitten, and I'll show you how much I like it," Michael growled, moving away briefly to push his pants down.

His shirt did not fare as well. Damn thing tore before he got it off his head. Fuck, he had never been so aroused in his life.

Her honeyed arousal seeped through the black cotton boxer briefs he wore, and fuck, it was all he could do to not come right there. Thick and hard, his cock throbbed against her, ready to penetrate her slick entrance, but not yet.

Michael growled, sucking on her tongue as he rocked his hips into her, loving the way she instinctively opened her legs wider.

Holy hell, she wants me.

The realization hit him like a slap to the face. He wanted to jump up and shout in triumph, but there was no way in fuck he was leaving his new favorite place.

Michael was not about to ruin or rush this. He slid his hand sup her body, taking time to explore every nuance and curve. She called herself plump, but she was mistaken. Kylie's body was a curvaceous wonderland designed to make a Tiger---in partic-ular *this Tiger*---lose his ever-loving mind.

"You're so big," she said, as he reached between them and pulled off his constrictive underwear.

Her eyes went wide, and Michael grunted in response. If she kept looking at his cock like that, this was going to be over before he began.

Fuck, no! His Tiger refused to go out like that. Michael went back to exploring her body, cupping her breasts in that crazy sexy little bra she wore. It was like a whisper of black fabric so sheer, it was hardly there. Tugging down each cup, he squeezed her puckered nipples while he explored her cleavage with his tongue, then grazed his teeth across one then the other.

"So beautiful," he growled, kneeling in front of her.

There was so much he wanted to do, he hardly knew where to start. And she was not idle, his sexy little mate had been touching him too. her hands ran over his chest and abs, her nails scratching his back and shoulders.

Fuck, it feels so good. She feels so good.

Her body was so hot, so soft, so fucking perfect. Michael leaned back, spreading her legs, loving that she let him. Kylie's eyes were bright, the celery green rimmed in the gold of her she-Cat. He paused a beat to take it all in.

Never had he seen someone that damn pretty. From the top of her golden head to the soles of her pink-polished feet. Her body was made for him, and the sight of her sex swathed in the tiny scrap of sheer black tulle made him just about lose his mind.

A little pink satin bow sat just above her cropped curls, matching the one between her fantastic breasts and giving just a hint of innocence to the sexy black confection. The effect was tantalizing, and Michael was blown away by another facet of her genius. He was ridiculously proud---not to mention, profoundly grateful---for both her amazing creativity and the fact he was the only man to see her modeling her own designs.

"God, you are really good at what you do," he said, and ran his hands up her body to show his appreciation.

"Thank you," she bit her lip and went to cover a tiny scar on her belly from his eyes.

Oh no, he was not having any of that. Michael narrowed his eyes. Time to show her just how beautiful she was.

Mine.

Chapter Nine

"D on't hide from me, Kylie," he begged. "I want to see all of you."

A shadow of worry marred her lovely face, but he would not allow that to linger long.

"I have scars from back then," she whispered.

"We all have scars. Yours just tell me how strong and fierce you are."

"But I, I mean, I have so many," she replied, her eyes wide and clear.

"So do I. Yours make so proud of who you are and what your survived. You're a warrior, my sweet Kylie. Of course, they also make me want to hunt down and destroy whoever did this to you---"

"Sweet, but she's gone now."

"Good for her. She's where she belongs. But more importantly, I want you to know our scars don't matter. We both have them, and they are part of us, but the only thing I want is to give you something better. *I* want to be better for you, Kylie, so we can have a life together."

"What do you mean? You don't even know me," she said, and he saw for the first time that was what bothered her.

"I know you, kitten. In here, I know everything I need to."

He took her hand and laid it against his chest just over his heart. The movement brought him closer to her. His big body loomed over hers and his hard, cloth-covered cock brushed against the apex of her thighs. He sucked in a breath at the sharp jolt of pleasure that stabbed through him at their new, intimate position.

"I never believed in fated mates," she told him as if it were some deep, dark secret, but Michael just smiled in response.

"We were told stories as cubs, but it was like a fairytale. But Kylie, make no mistake, you are my fated mate," he growled, catching her lip between his own, and tugging on it gently before he let it slide back out of his mouth. "By the time I am through tonight, you're gonna know it, too. Without. A. Single. Doubt."

Kylie purred. Her chest rumbled with it, and her eyes flashed green gold at him. The sound sent spikes of desire shooting through him like lightning strikes. Michael growled.

He took her face in his hands and started his sensual assault with a deep, soulful possession of her mouth that left the two of them panting and writhing against one another.

She'd missed out on a lot of things. Heavy petting and making out like teenagers in his childhood home seemed exactly right somehow.

"You taste so good, kitten. I can't get enough of you."

"Oh god! Do that again," she mewled as he flexed his hips, sending the hard ridge of his cock sliding against her soaked panties.

"Like wildflower honey laced with hot sauce," he groaned, licking a path down to her breasts.

Michael groaned aloud as he came face to face with the dusky pink tips. He leaned forward, sucking one plump nipple into his mouth.

Christ, she had superb breasts. He cupped them, kissed them, kneaded and pinched. He could just imagine pushing them together and sliding his cock between them. The image made him ache, but he put it away for later.

Kylie's fingers tangled in his hair, and he loved knowing she was losing herself to his touch. She purred and growled, and damn, but he paid close attention. He wanted to know what pleased her and committed every response and reaction to memory.

Unhooking her bra carefully, after all she had made it, he moaned as he caught her beautifully dusky-pink-tipped breasts in his hands. Teasing her nipples had been a treat before but holding them together and licking them both simultaneously was un-fucking-believable.

"Mine," he growled the word as he travelled further down her soft belly and moved her panties to the side, pressing his face to her slick folds.

"Michael!" she shouted at the first swipe of his tongue from her crack to her clit.

He loved the sound of his name falling desperately from her mouth. He wanted more of it, but he needed better access. Hands behind her knees, he pulled her down further on the sofa and held her legs apart.

"Sorry," he grunted, having no choice but to tear her panties clear off her hips.

"It's okay, I can make more. Just don't stop," she ordered him.

She was so sexy, biting her lip and watching him with those crazy gorgeous eyes. Michael held her gaze and opened his mouth, allowing his long tongue to snake all the way out. He swiped it slow and hard from her forbidden hole all the way up to her hooded clit and back down.

Again, and again, and again. Lick, swipe, nibble, suck.

He consumed every drop of her sweet nectar, swallowing it down, imprinting her unique flavors on his brain. The room was cool, but near her, he was on fire. Like his whole body was being swallowed by the flames of his need and her wanton abandon. Fuck, it was glorious.

"Michael, please, so close," she moaned, and her purring increased, vibrating throughout her entire body and his.

Tempting little minx gave him the most wonderful idea. He allowed his beast to come forward a trifle, and with his voice deep and rumbly, Michael told her exactly what he was going to do to her.

"Gonna make you come, kitten. First, I'm gonna stretch you with my fingers, fill your pussy so good, then I'm gonna lick you, and keep on licking you with the flat of my tongue. When I cover your sweet, needy little clit, I'm gonna growl, kitten. And I'm not stopping until you come all over my mouth. You want that, Kylie? Want me to make you come with my hands and my mouth?" he asked and waited for her assent.

Kylie nodded, and that was all he needed. Michael doubled his attention, kneading one breast with his free hand while slowly slipping one long finger inside her slick sheath.

Fuck.

His eyes crossed as her slick channel fought against him. She was small, so tight. Worry crossed his mind, but he dismissed it. She was his mate. She was made for him,

Her walls squeezed him as he bumped against her innocence. Slowly testing her limits, Michael continued to lick her tight bundle of nerves. He wouldn't hurt her, never that, but there was nothing he could do about the slight discomfort she would feel at first.

Kylie wiggled and rocked her hips in time with his ministrations, eager, and so fucking sweet, his dick was near to bursting. Precum soaked his boxer briefs, and he let go of her breast to give himself a tight squeeze. Michael growled deep, adding a much appreciated vibration to his actions.

"Come for me, baby," he grunted, allowing his Tiger more leeway and using his beast's purr to vibrate against her clit. He closed his mouth over the nubbin, sucking it into his greedy mouth.

"Don't stop, please," Kylie begged, her hands pulling on his hair. She lifted her hips, pressing her sex against his face. Close as she could get.

Michael loved it. Everything she did told him how she felt. He feasted on her. Sucking, purring, and growling against her pussy, fingering her sheath, and swallowing down every drop of her juices. Michael was determined to lick her all the way to paradise even if it killed him, he thought, but what a way to go!

Finally, Kylie exploded with a fierce cry. Her pussy rippled around his fingers, but Michael still wasn't finished. While she experienced her first of what he intended to be many orgasms that night, he reared up, freeing his cock from his underwear, he thrust his hips, taking her innocence when she would feel the least pain.

"Mine," he roared.

"Yes!" Kylie moaned, reaching up to grab onto him. She clung to his shoulders.

"Mine," she growled, and pulled him down to slam her mouth to his.

Michael's skin burned with need. His Tiger demanded he bite her now, claim her for all the world to see. But he held the beast in check. There was a proper time for that, after all. He swiveled his hips and pulled out of her viselike grip, just to slam back in again.

This was not the sweet, soft initiation he had intended, but Kylie didn't seem to mind. His Tiger pressed him, and he couldn't help but claim her with enthusiasm.

She grabbed his hips in her claw-tipped hands and scratched him, marking him there. Claiming him as hers, and *fuck*, his dick grew even harder.

"Mine," she growled that word again, sending his lust soaring.

Virgin that she was, his sexy little kitten was rocking his world. Kylie pushed up to meet his thrusts. The she-Tiger was right there with him, staking her claim and taking part in their mating.

Thank fucking God.

He held her face and bore his eyes into hers, wanting to see every single moment of them coming together. To record it in his mind for all eternity.

"Yes. Yours. And you are mine. Fuck, baby, you

feel like fucking perfection. Made just for me, Kylie, no one else. Mine," he growled.

"Yes. Fuck, yes. I want you to bite me, Michael, claim me. Now."

"I am, baby, in every way I can, I am claiming you tonight," he said, and growled as his words caused her pussy to clench around his cock.

Fuck, she was amazing. Her hands were every-where, stroking, kneading, scratching, even slapping. And he loved every fucking bit of it.

"I want it now," she growled impatiently, and bastard that he was, he chuckled.

"I'll give you everything you want, she-Cat, put my mark nice and high on your neck, but first I gotta feel your walls sucking my cock dry, can you do that? I need you to come for me."

"Wanna," she moaned.

"You will. Can you feel my cock, kitten? Feel me deep in that tight little pussy of yours?"

"Yes, yes, yes," she moaned, and he flipped them over so that she was astride him.

Taking her ass in his hands, he took control, bouncing and rocking her by that sweet peach of an ass. Michael lifted her up and slammed her down, harder and faster, he met her downward thrusts with his hips, burying his cock so deep he never wanted to leave.

Her she-Tiger was in control now, and she held onto his shoulders. Her eyes met his before tossing her head back giving him better access to those fantastic breasts of hers.

"That's it, baby," he grunted as he felt the first ripples of her orgasm begin to squeeze and caress his shaft.

"Fuck, yes, I claim you, Kylie, mate, I claim you right now," he roared and sunk his teeth in that spot just below her ear that he'd marked earlier.

Heat emanated from their bodies, and he swore the air itself sizzled. Michael's balls reared up and tightened as his dick exploded inside of her. Fuck, it was so good. So much better than anything else he'd ever experience.

He roared in surprise as pain erupted from his chest and he opened his eyes to see her blonde head lapping at the bite she'd just given him.

"Mine," she growled.

Thank fuck.

"Yours," he replied.

Chapter Ten

ho knew mating could be so much fun?

Kylie could hardly catch her breath. After their living room escapades, Michael had carried her to the bedroom.

There he'd laid her out on the *Tiger-king-sized bed* and proceeded to shock the shit out of her. The man was a doctor, so it was not surprising he knew about the female body. What was surprising was he knew exactly how to touch hers to make her lose her mind.

For example, Kylie had not been aware of her fantastic ability to experience pleasure at his hands, or mouth, *or even better*, his insatiable cock for hours on end. Of course, now, as she lay panting, she wondered if maybe he didn't break her vagina.

Oh fuck.

"What are you thinking about?" Michael's warm breath tickled her ear, and she wiggled her ass, burrowing close to his magnificent frame.

"I was wondering if you broke my pussy," she said honestly.

She allowed him to swallow her body with his embrace. Loving the feel of his deep chuckle as he kissed her head.

"Well, kitten, if I did, I promise to kiss it and make it better."

"You're insatiable."

Kylie tried to sound scandalized, but what came out was a sigh of anticipation. Nothing felt better than Michael's tongue on her sex, except for maybe his cock buried deep inside it.

"For you? Of course I am, kitten."

He chuckled again and tugged her till she was lying atop his warm, hard body. He couldn't seem to get enough of just holding her, and she loved it, especially the feeling of security being in his arms gave her.

Dammit, she was in love with him. Maybe she had been all along. Lord knew no one had ever made her feel this way. Like she was channeling a million lovely little surprise emotions with every touch, kiss, and caress.

Who knew she could be head over heels this quickly? She sighed happily in his arms, where she belonged.

"Seriously, I was thinking about that thing we did, where I sat on your lap and we both faced out towards the mirror. I swear, you went so deep inside me I saw stars," she murmured loving the way his breath caught.

Michael growled, hands cupping her ass, and she bit her lip as she felt his magnificent member stirring against her already wet sex.

"I liked that too. Especially the way your gorgeous breasts bounced up and down every time I filled your sweet pussy. You have the prettiest nipples, kitten."

Mm.

She moaned. Funny how much she liked it when he talked dirty to her. One big hand slipped down her crack and he teased her hole while the other wrapped around her hip. He pulled her up his body, sliding her along his length.

Kylie moaned, as he used her own slick folds to glide along his engorged cock. Fuck, he was huge. Shifters often were, or so she was told. But she had never felt this way with anyone else. Never wanted another man to touch her like this.

"Like that?" he whispered as he nuzzled her neck.

Fuck yeah, she liked that.

Unable to speak, she nodded, urging him to let her move faster, but he didn't. The fucker.

God, she loved the feel of his big arms wrapped around her and the strong, steady stroke of his dick along her slit. His thumb found her clit, and she grew even wetter.

"Guess my pussy isn't broken after all," she said on a moan as she became desperate for his penetration.

Instead of plunging deep like she wanted him to, Michael teased her instead. He rubbed the head of his cock along her entrance, coating himself in her juices, and driving her mad with need. She growled impatiently, wanting more.

"Michael," she moaned his name, and sat up, loving the feel of his thickness as it slid between her lips.

She felt his growl reverberate through him and into her, loved the press of his weight as he rolled them over and flipped her onto her belly. His thick fingers were strumming over her tiny little nubbin, and her stomach grew warm. Yes, this was what she wanted.

She felt him reach over to the nightstand and retrieve something, but she was almost too far gone to pay attention. The trickle of cool liquid seeped along her crack, and she moaned aloud as he rubbed it good and deep between her cheeks with his free hand. Then she felt something different.

With his fingers, Michael carefully teased and coated her hole, dipping one, then two thick digits inside and making her slick with oil. Kylie groaned against the intense fullness that filled her.

All the while, he kept strumming her clit, playing her like a maestro. Pleasure made her press back against him as her orgasm hovered just out of reach. Then he pressed the tip of his cock against her hole, and Kylie stilled.

That maddening hand continued to strum, bringing her to near ecstasy. Michael caged her in, and she felt his breath, ragged as her own, as he nipped her ear and whispered.

"Gonna claim you everywhere, Kylie. Gonna fill this sweet ass with my cum, mark you with my scent. Gonna tap this clit until you scream, and you're begging for my dick in your ass. Ready, kitten? Want me? Want my dick to fill your pretty ass?"

Kylie screamed as her orgasm ripped through her, spurred on by his dirty words. And he did not relent. Michael told her in graphic detail every single thing he'd planned to do to her, and fuck yes, he was right. She wanted all of it.

Right. Fucking. Now.

"Yes!" she moaned, and he growled, pressing his gorgeous cock into her ass.

He pushed his way inside of her until she was stretched so tight she thought she would burst. And he never stopped touching her. Through it all, his finger stroked and strummed.

"That's it, baby, take it, take me. You were made to take me," he growled. "Easy now, push back," he instructed, hissing when she obeyed.

Instinctively, she loosened her limbs for him, and he started to move---in and out, in short strokes at first, then longer ones.

Fuck, he felt good.

Her she-Tiger snarled and roared. The beast loved the feel of his thick cock buried in her ass. His fingers never stopped moving, and soon she was pushing back taking all of him with every thrust.

"That's good, kitten, so fucking good," he grunted and started moving in earnest.

Meting out a rhythm in a dance as old as time, Michael took her virgin ass as he had taken the rest of her. Every last bit was his. She could feel it in their *matebond* as it danced and pulsed around them, intensifying with each and every coming together.

She had been in denial since she'd met him. Had known even as she'd walked away and shaken her head that he was the only man she would ever want and need. The only man she'd ever give control of her body to. The only man she would ever love.

"Michael!" she screamed his name as the now familiar heat of bliss began to build and build until she was bucking eagerly back into his thrusts.

Taking more of him and demanding even more at every turn. Christ, she was a goddamn nympho for the man!

Her fangs descended, and she turned her head, nipping his arm with her teeth as he loomed over her, caging her in. With every flex of muscle, he took her to new and unreached heights, furthering her bliss.

He growled at her, taking her cue and marking her again on her shoulder. Fuck, but she lived for his mate mark, and the sweet orgasmic pleasure that rushed forward as he swallowed her blood and filled her with his seed.

Sex between Shifters was a wild, bloody, orgasmic affair, as she'd discovered. But what they had, this uncontrollable desire to be with one another, this communion between fated mates, was positively cataclysmic.

Michael panted above her, and they both moaned when he withdrew from her well-loved body.

"Mate," he grunted, leaning over to grab a cloth from the side table.

He wiped her clean and tucked her close to him. They would shower eventually. Had done so twice already, but she was too tired to move.

"Yes," she replied, nuzzling his flesh with her nose and lips.

Kylie had never felt quite this safe and satisfied in ever. For the first time, she was home. Happiness filled her as sleep finally overcame her willfulness to stay awake---and yes, at that point nothing else had kept her eyes open. But she was calm now, happy in her post-orgasmic state of bliss.

She had never felt as treasured as she did in his arms. It was something she'd wished for all her life. Even if he decided later, he didn't mean it. Even if this was only temporary.

No, she pushed away the negative vibes making her shiver and frown. They had no place here between them. Kylie would not allow those black thoughts to fill her, and instead, she listened to the steady beating of Michael's heart beneath her ear.

Mate.

T*he next day.*

"Good morning," Kylie said aloud, as she entered the Pride clinic early the next morning,

She had woken up alone, a note tucked beside her telling her that Michael had a patient to see. Kylie had grinned at the silly little heart he'd used with an M next to it as his signature.

She'd been surprised at having slept nearly twelve hours straight through the night. She never did that. Walking through the house to the hallway, she came to a locked door that opened into the medical clinic. Kylie grinned and pushed it open as she studied the framed pictures and smiled at the drawings his younger patients had sent him.

"Hey! Morning," her mate called back, coming out of a room to meet her.

His brilliant smile greeted her as he put down his patient's chart in the sleeve hanging on the door and stalked over to where she stood nervously in the entryway.

The clinic waiting room was empty, though she could hear someone in one of the patient rooms waiting for him, she supposed. Kylie allowed him to pull her close, and accepted his good morning kiss with gusto.

She sighed contentedly as he wrapped her in his arms, loving the way her head rested just beneath his chin. It was quickly becoming her favorite place in the world.

"Did you sleep well?" he asked.

"Too well," she answered.

"Ah, well, you earned a good rest," he said, and she could feel his smile as his cheek pressed against her hair.

It made what she was about to do even harder. She closed her eyes on the wave of sadness that threatened to overwhelm her.

Damn. She knew the moment he felt her pain and shivered at the speed with which his concern hit her in return.

"What's wrong?" he asked, and his anxious brown eyes met hers.

"Nothing, uh, I was just---"

She shrugged, wondering if this was a bad idea.

"We're a mated couple now, *mon petit chaton*. Remember, you can tell me anything," he said and touched her cheek with one long finger.

The result was a series of chills that ran down her back. Her she-Tiger wanted her to press herself fully against him and to never leave his side. After an entire day and night of lovemaking, she would have thought she'd had enough, but no.

Kylie could never have enough of Michael. He was the best damn man she'd ever seen. For the second time in the last two days, he'd rendered her speechless with words. The most incredible thing was how easily and readily she believed him.

Yes, they were mated now, and she knew she truly could tell him anything.

Almost anything.

Her heart hurt at the thought of what she had to do. But after hearing the message Uncle Uzzi had called and left on his answering machine, what choice did she have?

Oh Michael, she thought to herself. *I want to tell you.*

But how could she tell him she was leaving him for his own good and for the good of the Pride?

"Kylie?"

He whispered her name, more question than statement, and moved a step closer. The joviality left his voice, and, in that moment, they were more than man and woman or Tiger and she-Tiger, they were a mated pair---fated by the universe and destined for one another.

Desire pulsed between them, a living, breathing thing that demanded the right to grow, to be allowed to thrive, and damn, but Kylie wanted it to have the chance.

She wanted him---oh how she wanted him. But she couldn't be selfish that way.

"Michael---"

She gripped his shirt in her hands, wrinkling the soft material, and noted the subtle change in his masculine fragrance. It was a heady combination of his male musk and spearmint leaves, the kind she used to pick outside in the abandoned gardens near the holler. Her father used to tuck the leaves behind her ear when she was a child running barefoot through the woods.

That was a happier time. Before her mother had come into her life and changed the course of things with her cruelty. Before Waylon and his streak of uncouth Tigers had destroyed the Sharp Claw Pride with their greed.

No.

She couldn't allow them to come to Maverick Point and wreak their havoc on this place she'd grown to call home. She could not put the people she loved in danger. Kylie would risk no one being hurt.

No. Especially not him.

"Dr. Mikey!" a child's voice called from the examination room, causing the couple to split apart, and giggle as if they were a couple of teenagers caught making out.

She realized two people were inside the examination room. The small boy and his mother---his Tiger Shifter mother.

"Yes, Paulie. I'm coming," Michael smiled and turned to greet his small patient.

Kylie smiled at the happy cub's voice and turned to say hello to him as well. Paulie was about five-years old with dimples and chubby cheeks. He had dark hair and eyes, and had obviously just lost a tooth. His little pink tongue kept poking through the hole even as he called for his doctor.

"Sorry, doc, I have to get to work, if we can get

on with his shot?" Pamela Brown stuck her head out of the doorway.

The thin woman's eyes were smiling when they'd landed on her son, but they widened in fear when she saw Kylie.

After what she'd done, Kylie wasn't exactly the female's biggest fan. She had to admit, seeing the woman so close to her mate had her inner she-Tiger snarling and snapping her jaws.

Oh my! I'm jealous, she thought with wonder.

"Of course, give me one second with my mate, please, Pamela," Michael replied, but his eyes never left Kylie.

Pamela was watching her, too. She looked scared and nervous, swallowing audibly before she remembered herself. Instinctively, the too thin female stepped out of the room, her hand on her son's shoulder as she tucked him quickly behind her.

"Paulie, come here," she said in a scared voice that made Kylie's heart squeeze.

"Mama, Doc Mikey's got a mate!" the boy exclaimed cheerfully.

"Yes, so he does," she smiled at her son. "Let's leave them alone a moment, and wait in the room--
-"

"Did you say I gots to get a shot?" his lower lip

trembled, and Pamela knelt in front of him, hands on his cheeks.

"Yes, I did, but I promise I will be there with you and hold your hand."

"Don't want it," he shook his head as big tears formed. "Mama, I don't wanna get shot!"

"Hey, Paulie, you don't have to worry. It's not that kind of shot," Michael's voice dripped with sympathy even as the boy tried to pull away from his mother.

"Hi there," Kylie said, stepping towards the boy and crouching down to his level. "I'm Kylie. Did you say your name is Paulie?"

Kylie began looking up at his mother, and Pamela looked away, but she remained in front of him, protecting the small boy.

Good mom, Kylie thought, impressed by the she-Tiger's maternal instincts.

At first, she was annoyed the woman thought Kylie would ever hurt a cub, but then the truth hit her. This was Pamela's son, and she was behaving as any mother would. Any mother, except hers, of course.

Paulie Brown was an innocent and a sweet cub. His mother might have done some bad things in her life, but mostly she'd had bad things done to her. She was a victim, and Kylie knew that now. Even if she didn't, the boy had nothing to do with any of the woman's past.

It was truly mind boggling. Pamela had a son. Why had she never seen him? And who was the daddy?

Not my business, she thought.

And it was true, it didn't matter. Paulie was an innocent and he should be loved and protected by all members of the Pride. Including her, she realized, and smiled at him.

"Pamela?" Michael spoke, breaking the awkward silence. "Allow me to formally introduce you to my mate, Kylie McNaughton."

Michael then knelt down to speak to the boy, using his best doctor's voice. Kylie was impressed.

"Paulie, the last time you were here, we spoke about what was going to happen on your next visit. Do you remember?"

"Yes, I member," the child replied. "But I changed my mind. I don't want no shots!"

The boy pulled away from his mother's hand and ran across the room, away from the adults. Pamela moved to chase him, and so did Michael, but Kylie stilled them both with a shake of her head. She pressed her forefinger to her lips and walked across the room. She crouched down in front of where he was hiding behind the curtains.

"So, the reason why I asked about your name was because I heard of a famous Paulie, and I was wondering if you were related," she said, aware of the other two adults listening in keenly.

"A famous Paulie?" the little boy replied, his voice muffled by the thick fabric curtain.

"That's right. This famous Paulie was really big. Taller and wider than any other man in the land. Why, they say he could cut down a full grown pine tree with one swing of his ax!"

"No way!" Paulie said and hiccupped.

"Way," Kylie told him. "He was so strong he could cut down more trees in a day than ten men---"

"But cutting trees is bad, isn't it?"

"Well, at the time it was the only job around. Like your pal Mikey is a doctor, this Paulie was a lumber-jack. And guess what?"

"What?"

"Well, he was so big and strong, there wasn't a horse big enough to carry him! So, he rode a blue oxen named Babe."

"Wow! Can I meet him?"

"I'm afraid not. This happened a long time ago, back when logging was a huge industry," she said.

"What's logging?" Paulie asked, peeking out from behind the curtain.

"It's when folks cut down trees for useful things like building railroads and houses. Nowadays we have to be really careful to take care of our planet though," she told the boy in a calm, quiet-like voice.

Kylie was still crouched down, but she did not have long to wait. The small cub crept out from behind the curtain, his head cocked to the side.

"You mean like *Earfth Day?*" he said, and she nodded and smiled at his mispronunciation.

"That's right?"

"So, who's this famous Paulie? He got a last name?"

"He sure does. Haven 't you ever heard of Paul Bunyan?" Kylie asked and walked him back to the examination room, she signaled with her hand behind her back for the other adults to follow.

"Come on, Mama! You too, Doc Mikey. Your mate's gonna tell us more about a famous Paulie," the cub said and waved them over.

Kylie began telling the story of the larger than life American folk hero while Michael measured and weighed and readied the young cub's booster shot. Paulie was so engrossed in her story, he hardly did more than wince when Michael gave him the dreaded needle.

As soon as he was finished, he wanted to play a game pretending he was *Paul Bunyan* riding *Babe the Blue Ox*. Michael readily accepted the challenge and dropped to his knees bellowing like some kind of hurt cow, but Kylie had to give him props.

He was wonderful. Michael even gave the boy a ride around the empty office while the two women smiled and cheered them on.

Kylie laughed at their playful antics and her she-Tiger pressed against her mind. She purred softly and approvingly of her mate's activities. He was going to make an excellent father to their cubs.

If she stuck around and got the chance to find out. But she wouldn't. Not if she left him.

"Okay, Paulie, that's enough for now. You did a good job, buddy! Pamela, just give me a second to get you the paper you need for his return to school," Michael told the mother, nothing but professional as he spoke.

When he turned to Kylie with glittering dark eyes, she saw heat and more in his gaze. The jealousy she had felt earlier was gone. No matter what, Michael was serious about her being the only one for him. She would be a fool to waste this chance.

"Wait for me?" he asked.

"Sure," she said.

"Thank you for the story, Mrs. Doc Mikey," Paulie said and giggled.

"Yes," Pamela added, holding her son's hand, "Thank you."

"No problem. He's a very sweet boy," she said, and watched as Pamela's usually hard face softened for a moment.

"He's my whole life," she said honestly.

And Kylie felt the truth in her words. It seemed she had been very wrong about the she-Cat. True, Pamela had not made life easy for Kylie's friends, but the woman had been a victim of abuse.

She had been seriously wronged, and if Gretchen could forgive her---even more than that, she was trying to help the female---then Kylie had no cause to spread any more grief around.

Kylie watched her talk to her son, and Pamela did really look good, she thought to herself. Better somehow, like she was healthier than she had when Kylie had first arrived in Maverick Point. Maybe Gretchen was right, and the woman deserved a second chance.

"Here you go," Michael came in, and handed Pamela an envelope.

"Thanks," she said, and nodded awkwardly.

She was dressed in a neat pair of jeans with a long-sleeved blouse that was at odds with how she used to look, Kylie realized. She seemed to have put on weight, and it agreed with her. She was softer somehow. And that couldn't be a bad thing.

Pamela and Paulie both waved goodbye before heading outdoors to the overwhelming New Jersey summer heat.

Michael quickly closed the door behind them and stalked over to his mate. He placed both hands on her hips and brought his forehead down to touch hers.

A sense of perfect harmony and peace, along with a bone deep need for the man, had her inner Tiger rearing up and pushing Kylie to mash herself to him.

The rock-hard evidence of his own echoing desire pressed against her soft belly and a resounding purr built in her throat.

"Mate," he nuzzled her face until his lips found hers, capturing them in a soul-searing kiss that had them both breathless in seconds.

"We can't do this now," she moaned, but zippers and buttons were hurriedly opened and a moment later, Michael had her half-naked and against the cool, painted wall.

"I locked the door," he murmured as he lifted her up and found her with his throbbing manhood.

Legs splayed with her jeans dangling from one foot and his glorious cock buried between her slick folds, Kylie moaned and clung to him as Michael suckled her nipple, biting the hard nubbin while he pumped his hips.

She all but melted as he pressed deep inside, claiming her body with the same miraculous strength he had all through the night before.

And early that morning too.

His need was as great as her own, she realized with a shiver that raced down her spine all the way to where they were joined. *Fuck*, she loved the way he filled her.

"Mine," he grunted as he drove her mindless with desire.

He was wild and rough, relentless in his pursuit of their mutual and undeniable pleasure. And yet, Michael was breathtakingly tender, and *oh so careful*. Even cradled the back of her head with his hands to keep her from banging it as he slammed his hips into hers, essentially fucking her stupid.

And wasn't that just positively delicious?

Her entire body sizzled. She was no longer in control of her actions, no, Kylie was a puppet dancing to his tune. His mastery of her body proved her complete undoing.

"Gonna come," she moaned, scratching at his shoulders underneath his opened shirt.

That just made him all the more eager to please her. His muscles rippled and he worked harder. Fucking her sublimely with that body she loved so much. His bulk was typically hidden behind nicely made clothes and impeccable manners, which was why she had damn near swallowed her tongue the first time she saw him standing naked as the day he was born. And when he was like this, raw and out of control, Kylie was a certified goner.

He was so fucking gorgeous. Especially when he was fucking her, she thought with a somewhat crude and wicked grin.

"More," she growled, squeezing her thighs tight around his narrow waist.

He growled but complied, giver that he was, strumming her clit with one hand while his dick did magnificent things to her. Each stroke of his veined shaft sent tendrils of unparalleled pleasure spiking through her blood.

She could see it just there, hovering in the near future. That glorious gift of the perfect release that only her mate could give her.

"Want," she murmured. "Need," she cried.

"Now," he commanded.

And that was all it took. A gruff demand from her sexy as fuck mate, and finally, it was hers. Kylie came hard, screaming his name. She roared her fulfillment, biting him again on his neck, and Michael bellowed in turn.

He filled her with his cum, mashing his hips to hers and pressing his pubis against her needy clit. Stars exploded behind her eyes, and her pleasure went on and on, spiraling into infinity.

Amber gold eyes watched her, and Kylie's beast surged forward. She finally released her hold on his skin, fangs receding, as she lapped at the wound, sealing it, and dropping a soft kiss to apologize for the hurt.

Typically, one bite would do, but over the last day and a half she quickly realized they'd given each other half a dozen mating marks minimum. Whatever happened, she wouldn't be going anywhere.

Her she-Tiger wouldn't allow it. She knew that, and finally, she accepted it. Their matebond flexed and pulsed around them, wrapping them both in a cocoon of love and Shifter magic.

Shit. She loved the man. Like truly, madly, deeply in love.

The realization was powerful even as they remained locked in place. Working hard to regain their breaths, she almost did not hear it when a knock sounded at the door.

"Hold on," Michael yelled, and turned back, kissing her lips before he eased out of her.

She was wobbly on her feet, but he helped her stand and even wound up half-dressing her. Kylie was too cock-stunned to move. She'd understood it when he'd claimed her that he had been hers from the start, but Kylie had not acknowledged what that truly meant until right now.

Fated mates.

A fairytale for Shifters, but real too. She had found hers. Even more, she loved him. Like that head over heels, sappy movie, and awful country music kind of love. Kylie laughed softly, and he cocked his head to the side as he righted his own clothes.

"What is it?"

"Nothing," she said, and nodded towards the door where someone was pounding away.

"Coming," he growled.

"We did that already," she snarked, and he did a double take.

"Feisty little kitten," he grinned and winked at her.

"I hate to go, but I have patients," he said as he went to the door, but she was already nodding.

"And I have to get ready for the baby shower," she replied.

"I'll see you there later?"

"Yes. Of course," he said. "And Kylie?"

"Yeah?"

"I don't want you to worry yourself thinking to death about this all day, but I thought you should know---"

"Know what?" she asked, retying her sneaker.

"I love you."

Chapter Eleven

Kylie left Michael to tend his patients and waited for her ride outside the house. She had left her car at the Pride House the night before. She hadn't thought about it before, but retrieving the vehicle was going to be mortifying.

Not her fault. She simply had not been thinking about it or how she would get anywhere the next day.

Duh, said her she-Tiger.

All she'd been thinking about was getting her hands on a very naked Michael Turner. The Pride Healer had spent the whole night initiating her into the sensual side of mating.

Thank fuck, she'd lucked out in that department.

Michael was an exceptional lover. Not that she'd

had anything to compare him to, but she knew it without a doubt. She frowned as a smiling Hank held the rear passenger door open for her, as she climbed into the limo that had arrived to pick her up.

"Good morning, dear. You missed quite the pre-party last night," he began.

"Oh crap, is Elissa terribly upset?"

"Not at all. Everyone is looking forward to the shower today, but I heard some of the ladies say you are not getting away without a performance---"

"Oh Lord, not karaoke! What do I have to do to make them just give up on me already?"

"Kylie, my dear, I do not think anyone here will ever do that," he replied, his blue eyes glowing with magic. "Now, tell me, how are you feeling today?"

Uncle Uzzi smiled as he sat across from Kylie in the immaculate car, and she tried to wrap her head around everything the older man had just said. She wanted to believe his words were true, but did not think she could bear to find out they weren't.

Just the fact she was allowed in the Maverick Pride was too good for words, but to be treated like an old friend by members of the inner circle was incredibly humbling. She had been alone for so long.

Kylie realized she would give anything to truly belong.

"I'm feeling okay, thanks," Kylie returned, and tried to ignore the blush warming her cheeks.

It was hard to pretend not to be embarrassed when she knew the Witch knew what she had been up to. Kylie bit her lip nervously. Should she or shouldn't she ask this man what to do about her current situation?

"Hank? Can you run us down to *Jessica's Closet*? I promised I'd pick her up as well," Uncle Uzzi instructed the driver before turning his electric blue eyes on the young woman.

"You know, it's not that I can't drive, but I do prefer to use Hank's livery service when I am visiting the Garden State. There's just something about his old world courtesy that reminds me of the old days," Uzzi told Kylie conspiratorially.

"I bet," Kylie said.

The handsome chauffeur was something else alright. She smelled fowl on him, but was unsure what type of Bird Shifter he was. He had great manners, and his limo was always immaculate. She and the girls used to giggle over how hot he looked in his uniform, but handsome as he was, he did nothing for Kylie.

Not like a certain hot doctor, she might add.

"Well, now, I suggest you ask me whatever it is that's on your mind, Kylie McNaughton. While we have the time."

"Oh, uh," she wiggled in her seat and closed her eyes for a count of three.

The shameful truth was a bit embarrassing, but she had to admit it to someone. Kylie ran a hand over her hair and hoped it wasn't too disheveled from her romp with Michael.

Michael. Mate.

Her silly she-Cat went belly up just thinking about the dang man. Especially the way he'd looked in various positions and when he'd whispered deliciously naughty things to her.

Sigh.

How was she supposed to concentrate when images of the spectacularly raunchy things he'd introduced her to, kept popping up in her mind?

"Kylie? Well, if you won't talk, then allow me to state that we have five minutes before we pull up outside of *Jessica's Closet*. Once we get there, I suggest a change of clothes, or the Neta, Nari, and every Shifter within ten feet of you will be sure to pick up on exactly what you and Michael have been up to this morning."

Though his words were casual, Uncle Uzzi eyed her disheveled wardrobe with amusement twinkling in his sapphire gaze. Kylie felt her cheeks heat up, and embarrassment coursed through her.

"Oh my Lord! I am so sorry, Uncle Uzzi," she said, horrified.

"Nonsense. I was a married man too and believe me when I tell you my *liebling* and I were quite inseparable. She was quite the believer in physical intimacy, was what kept a marriage strong, while the heart kept it warm."

"That sounds so romantic," she told him.

"Now, are you sure you have nothing else to say?"

"Well, I guess I should just tell you the truth. You see, I heard the message you left about the Sharp Claw Pride closing in on me, and I wondered if things would not be better for everyone here if I just left," she whispered the last word, scared her confession would reveal her as the selfish coward she was.

Kylie's eyes filled with tears, and she took the tissue Uncle Uzzi offered.

"Kylie, you leaving is ---" he began, but Kylie cut him off.

"Uncle Uzzi, I know I should leave for everyone's sake, but I don't think I can," she cried miserably.

"This is the first place I ever felt like I belonged. I

want it too much. I want *him* too much. Does that make me selfish?"

"Kylie, I am surprised at you! Of course, it does not make you selfish to want to be happy, loved, and safe, and you are all those things here, aren't you?" Uzzi asked, sympathy shining in his eyes.

"I think so," she murmured. "Am I supposed to love him so much, so fast?"

"Love is good, no? It is the purpose of life."

"I guess, I mean, I don't have a lot of experience with love. But I always knew Michael was something special to me."

"Indeed, he is your fate, child."

"Fated mates?"

"Of course, dear."

"It seems so strange," she whispered. "I mean, that sort of thing seemed to be for other people. Not me. Never me." Kylie closed her eyes, took a deep breath, and tried to shake off the feeling of impending doom.

Wasn't it time she embraced a little hope? Maybe Uzzi was right. Maybe she needed to just trust in the Fates, or more precisely, in the fact that Michael was her fated mate.

"What do I do if he decides he doesn't want me anymore?"

Kylie looked down at her short-clipped nails and gave voice to her biggest fear. She had learned to be a realist before she had ever come to Maverick Point. Always expecting the worst was second nature.

Her childhood had allowed for nothing else. Dreaming about fairytales was not something that was encouraged. Images of a lonely little girl flashed through her brain until the little girl grew into a terrified teen, and then finally, a woman on the run who'd managed to find a place to land.

Maverick Point had become more than just that, though. She'd made friends there, started a business, and found her mate. Kylie had a home now.

"There is no way Michael Turner does not want you, child. Are you not aware of the months he's spent pining for you? The Tiger has been waiting for the right moment to claim you, but you never have to settle. You know this, right? You are worth a king's ransom, child, but should he not make you happy---"

A warm, wrinkled hand closed over hers and she looked up to see Uncle Uzzi's eyes brimming with emotion. Kylie clasped his hand in return, knowing finally why he was everyone's *uncle*. The man had more kindness in his pinky than any relative she had ever had. He was like family, and she was grateful for him.

"Oh no, Uncle Uzzi, he makes me so very happy. Truth is, I was ready to run today, but after talking to you, I think this is where I belong. I love Michael. He told me he loved me before I left his office. But he wasn't even looking at me. He just said it, real casually---"

"Well, maybe he did not want to frighten you."

"Maybe," she agreed. "Anyway, I think I loved him since the first day I saw him. I know he's a doctor but I'm just me, and, well---"

"We will have none of that now, my dear child. And don't you ever let me catch you saying anything like that again," Uzzi said, and she could tell he was simmering with outrage.

"Who told you formal education made a person good or better than anyone else? Why, some of the finest people I know do not even know how to read," Uzzi started.

"A medical degree does not make a person better than you. Especially not you, my dear Kylie---You are a warm, kind, beautiful woman. A fierce, protective, brave she-Tiger. Not to mention, a completely brilliant designer, if I do say so myself. I have even started passing your cards out to my clients, and so far, they love your work," Uzzi informed her.

"Oh!" Kylie was surprised by Uzzi's statement, and she laughed, wiping a tear from her eye. "Thank you for your endorsement."

"Of course but believe me I would not tell anyone about your wares if they were not good. The mates of my clients are too precious for subpar handling, my dear, and *Kisses by Kylie* knows how to treat today's woman or, so I have been told," Uzzi stated.

"Back to you and Michael. Your love for each other will only grow, Kylie. It's how these things are meant to be."

"Oh, but what if he only thinks he loves me," she began, then stopped and stared at Uncle Uzzi, her mouth hanging open. "Wait, he does, doesn't he? He really loves me," she said with wonder lacing every word.

"Yes, dear, of course he loves you. He's no dummy. Now, go run up to your apartment while I get Jessica, quick shower and change, then meet me back down here in fifteen minutes," the older Witch instructed and winked.

"Good idea. I'll be right with y'all," Kylie said, and she didn't even wince when a bit of South Carolina poured into her voice.

She took the stairs two at a time, hardly aware of her surroundings and so full of hope, more than she'd allowed herself to feel in years.

Kylie wondered if this was what euphoria felt like. She was in love, and even better, someone loved her back. Eyes twinkling, she grinned with amusement as she thought about all the shenanigans she and Michael had gotten up to in the hours since he'd brought her home from the Pride House.

Kylie unlocked the door that led to the stairwell to her apartment. It was unusually dark and quiet, but she was too busy daydreaming over her night with Michael. The things he'd done to her untried body. Kylie had never had time for sexual exploration.

Shifters were very physical creatures, but she had spent so much of her childhood and young adulthood just trying to make it out of her old Pride alive, She'd never had a boyfriend. Never knew what being in love meant, physically speaking.

To say she'd been shocked was an understatement. Michael had done things to and with her, she'd only ever read about. He made her quiver and sigh, moan and scream, gasp and come louder and harder than any battery-operated boyfriend from her intimate toy collection.

Michael Turner was something of a sex god, in her opinion. He'd been completely insatiable, licking and fucking her into oblivion. And Kylie had loved every minute of it. Honestly, she'd never felt like more of a woman than when she'd been wrapped up in his arms, and his kiss, with his big, beautiful body between her thighs.

She'd always worried about her size. Her old Pride had teased her mercilessly for being short and plump, but Michael did not seem to mind. He'd soon laid all her fears to rest by showing her just how much he liked her curvy little frame.

Thank God.

"Hello, Kylie," a harsh voice reached her ears.

Kylie stopped with her foot midair as a villain from her past came into view. His heavy footsteps as he pushed off the wall, leaving the shadows where he'd been hidden, were like thunder in her ears.

Fear raced up her spine, and suddenly she was a teenaged girl again, bleeding and broken and waiting to die at the hands of her own mother and the Pride that should have loved her. The bastard sneered, liking her fear and Kylie growled a warning.

"Still the same, Kylie. Short and fat, and too stupid to live, ain't ya, girl?"

Her fear exploded, but she realized it wasn't for

herself. It was for everyone she loved. She swallowed down hard and looked up, knowing it was too late to stop this from happening.

He'd found her.

Waiting at the top of the landing was Waylon Pitt. He wore the same scraggly-looking beard as he'd had three years earlier, and his scent was positively unmistakable. She scrunched up her nose, barely stopping herself from covering it with her hands. He was older, uglier, and smellier than ever as he stepped out of the shadowed hall.

Good Lord, she wondered how she hadn't noticed it before. Her she-Tiger snarled at his approach, but the cretin wheezed a laugh.

"Guess that cloaking spell I bought really worked, didn't it, girl? Didn't even see me comin', did ya?" Waylon spit on the hallway floor, and Kylie jerked in revulsion.

"What do you want?" Kylie bit out the question, backing down a step.

The sounds of someone behind her had her head whipping around, and she startled. A younger male Tiger, one she did not recognize appeared, and he had a shotgun in his hands.

Fuck.

Kylie was surrounded and there was no way she

could call for help. Not with these two assholes armed and dangerous.

"I want what I always wanted---what I deserve! I want the Sharp Claw Pride, and you are gonna get it for me!" Waylon hissed, spitting his stink all over the place.

"No, I am not, Waylon. Whatever you might think, I have nothing to do with that Pride, and they have never had anything to do with me. I am not my mother's daughter. Those people won't follow you because of me."

"That's bullshit! Key to the Pride is with the heir. You *are* your mother's daughter," he growled, reaching over, and grabbing her arm with his claw-tipped hands.

"You can't do this!"

"Who's gonna stop me, girl? I'll have ya now like I shoulda had ya then!"

"No! I'm already mated," she cried out, but he was already pulling her up the stairs and pressing his foul-smelling body against hers.

"I'll fuck him right out of you. Fill you with my cum and cover your mate mark with my own," Waylon snarled, and she could see the craziness in his eyes.

More spittle and filth flew from his mouth,

causing more of his stink to reach her. She could not help herself, she gagged. Waylon grinned slowly at her discomfort. His gaze never left hers as he squeezed her forearm, drawing blood.

Kylie whimpered, wanting to shy away from his touch and his feral eyes. They glowed a sickly yellow color that attested to his warped state of mind. The other Tiger behind her pressed the gun into her spine, making it impossible for her to retreat.

"Think about this, Waylon. My Neta's sister is right below us. She'll hear," Kylie pleaded, hoping she was right, and trying desperately not to gag on the stench of both lust and loathing that seemed to leak from the unworthy male.

"*I* am your Neta," he growled, and before she could do anything else, Waylon lunged for her.

Kylie's scream got stuck in her throat. She tried to move, but only her eyes seemed to obey and when she looked down, she saw why.

A syringe was sticking out of her arm, and the plunger was pushed all the way down. Green residue clung to the plastic, but the bulk of it was now swimming in her veins.

"That potion will take the fight right outta ya, little girl. We'll have an old-fashioned claiming in front of the whole Pride when we get back home. I'll fuck ya and bite ya, and I will become the Neta for real. You and me, see we belong together, Kylie. Let's go," he snarled

She tried to struggle as he gave his accomplice instructions, but her limbs were frozen. She couldn't talk, couldn't move, not an inch. Breathing was hard, and when Waylon grabbed her to him, harshly squeezing her breast before tossing her over his shoulder like a side of beef, she thought she was going to puke.

Michael! His face was the only thing in her mind as the bastard stole her from the hallway. She felt tears fall from her frozen, unblinking eyes.

The world seemed to turn round, and she realized he'd opened a window and was climbing down the fire escape with her over his shoulder, like so much dead weight, which she supposed she was.

Fuck. How the hell was she supposed to escape?

"Move," Waylon growled at his minion. "Start the truck, we need to go now before these city Cats get any ideas."

Well, that was just great.

Kylie had to abandon all hope of being seen and rescued by Hank, Uncle Uzzi, or even Jessica. She wanted to scream, but couldn't, still caught in the semi-paralyzed state from the sludge he had injected into her veins.

Her body was immobile, but her mind was racing. She tried not to panic as the two sorry excuses for Tiger Shifters hustled down the ladder and raced around the back of the building to an old beat up pick-up truck.

Waylon tossed her into the cab, forcing her between them. She would have fallen face first into the dashboard if the asshole minion hadn't grabbed her by the hair to pull her back. She should probably thank the fucker, but could no longer speak. Whatever foul magical concoction Waylon had forced on her, she was now completely paralyzed. Stuck between two disgusting males in a broken down truck littered with fast food wrappers and empty beer cans, Kylie cursed her luck.

How am I going to get out of this?

Every single molecule that made up her being was intent on escaping and getting back home to Michael and the Maverick Pride. Waylon was a lowlife, but he was obviously on the outs with her mother's old set of leaders.

Otherwise, the fucker would not be there with that single scrawny excuse for a male. Where was his original group of cronies? She had to admit, this surprised her.

He must be fighting everyone for a place in the Pride and the ultimate position as Neta. The younger male with him was probably someone she knew, and for a moment she hoped to reason with him.

With her next breath, she concentrated on filtering out the flavors but came up blank. If this was someone from the Sharp Claw Pride, then she didn't know him. All she could do was sit and wait while they drove out of town.

Kylie looked at the image of Mount Maverick in the rearview mirror and wanted to scream at the injustice of it all. It was that image that had called to her when she had been on the run. That mountain that had seemed so strong and still in the madness of it all. Had she not seen it, she might not have made the decision to stop in the tiny New Jersey town.

But like Uncle Uzzi said, it was fate. Mount Maverick grew smaller in her rearview, but she was hopeful it would not be the last time she saw it. That image stayed with her as the miles grew longer, leading her away from her true Pride, and her fated mate.

The cruelty of her reality was almost too much to

bear. She had so much to live for now, but she would rather die than allow Waylon to make good on his promise to taint her.

"Don't worry," sneered Waylon, as if he'd been privy to her inner dialogue. "I'll get his stink off ya real soon, girl."

He leaned over and licked her cheek, and she damn near vomited in her mouth.

No! Dear gods, no.

Fear and pain sliced through her as sure as a sword. Her heart was breaking, and as it crumbled into pieces, the poor, abused muscle cried out for her mate.

Michael, please hear me, please know I love you. I have always loved you.

Kylie tried not to shudder as Waylon leaned over again and nipped her ear between his teeth.

"You gonna fuck her soon, Waylon?" the young male asked.

"That's Neta, asshole!"

"Right, uh, you gonna fuck her soon, *Neta?*"

The two males started laughing and Kylie wanted to scream. She scented lust and something worse, an evil sort of frenzy that she had never encountered. Her she-Tiger snarled, wanting to come forward, but she could only recoil in the metaphysical plane where she waited.

For some reason, Kylie was unable to call the beast all the way forward. She was trying to find their link through the veil that lead to the plane where her Tiger usually rested until called, but it was like she was hidden in a mist of sorts.

"Don't bother your kitty now, girl. That shot won't let her play. Not till after I show her who's boss," Waylon explained, yanking her head back by her hair.

What the fuck was with these assholes and her ponytail?

Stars exploded behind her eyes, and she felt the start of a migraine coming down on her. It was unusual for Shifters to have them, but now and then, Kylie suffered terribly.

"Get your she-Cat under my thumb, rough as I gotta be, ya hear? By then you'll have learned to like it," he grunted and lifted her hand, licking it with his slimy tongue.

Her stomach roiled, and Kylie wanted to ask how that was even possible. Cats did not have slimy tongues, theirs were dry and perfect. But not him. Something was wrong with Waylon. Something other than the obvious.

"Give it to her now," he ordered, squeezing her arm and she startled, realizing she had been struggling in his grasp.

"Yes, Wayl-, *er*, Neta," the young moron replied.

Kylie struggled harder, but the younger Tiger was not nearly as agreeable as Waylon. He slapped her hard, splitting her lip, and she cried out in pain. It felt good to make a sound, though she hurt like hell.

"Do not fucking touch her again! She is mine!" Waylon bellowed, and she winced at his roar.

"Sorry about that, girl. Ignore Boris here. Now, this second shot should make ya feel real nice, and compliant like."

"In ya go," the crazed youth said as he pushed the needle into her vein.

The sludge stung as it went in, and tears rolled down her face, but Kylie continued to focus on the rearview mirror. There was no way she was going to allow herself to be used for this man or any other to rule a Pride that had never done anything but hurt her.

She would die first. If that was going to happen, she wanted the last thing she remembered to be something good. The shadowy image of Mount Maverick was almost still visible, or maybe it was her imagination, but either way, she kept on staring.

It was the only place she'd finally felt as if she'd belonged, and if she had a choice, it would be the only place she went home to.

I'm so sorry for everything we won't get to do, Michael, she thought one last time before darkness took her.

Chapter Twelve

"What do you mean, she's gone?" Michael roared and paced Hunter's office.

Brayden stood behind the Neta, just to his right, as was his place as Pride Beta. Uncle Uzzi was looking worried in his seat in front of his desk with Jessica holding his hand. The two of them had been in *Jessica's Closet*, waiting for Kylie to finish changing her clothes, so they could come over and help with the final setup for Elissa's baby shower, that was to take place in just an hour.

They had all been working hard to make the event a special one for the heavily pregnant Nari. The Alpha fem had not been told of the events and he understood, after all, her condition was delicate.

And yet, he could not control the way his beast snarled and snapped, feeling as though he were breaking in two.

His mate was missing, and he didn't have a clue why or where she'd gone. The others looked at him strangely. They did not understand, but Michael knew Kylie. She would not leave him, especially not after last night.

"Look, she's always been distant. Maybe she just left, bro," Brayden offered quietly.

"No," Michael ran a hand over his face.

He knew he'd been high-handed when he'd taken the *Ancient Rite of Proclamation* to claim his mate, but he thought he'd persuaded her last night that it was the right move. After what they'd shared, and the way she responded to him, Michael had assumed she was every bit as infatuated as he.

Fuck that.

It was more than infatuation. He loved the woman. She was his one true and fated mate. The single most important person to him in the entire universe.

"Pierce and the guys have been over her apartment, they found nothing there. I am sorry, but it looks like she just bailed," Brayden insisted.

"Brayden," Jessica hissed a warning to her mate.

It was a good thing too, because Michael's beast was spoiling for a fight, and the big Bear would do more than suffice. Everyone always assumed that because he was always *the nice guy*, Michael was, therefore, weak.

But he was not weak. He had a seven hundred pound Tiger inside of him who would take on the challenge of a Bear with relish if it got him his mate back. But it wouldn't, and that was the only thing that stopped him from attacking him just then.

Shit.

Brayden was his friend, not his foe. Michael knew that, but his beast was itching to break free.

He wanted her back. Wanted to know she was safe.

"I don't believe she would just leave, Michael," inserted Uncle Uzzi. "Kylie had been speaking very highly of what transpired yesterday between you two. No details," he added. "But I know she was looking forward to developing her relationship with you."

"Thank you," Michael mumbled, sparing the older Witch a glance.

Shame rose like bile as he wondered in the tiniest crevice of his mind if maybe Brayden wasn't right after all. Kylie had not exactly chosen him as a mate. He'd forced it on her.

Shit. Fuck. Damn.

He was, at best, a bully, and at worst, *well*, he didn't even want to consider it. All he knew now, was that he loved her, and wanted her safe. If she wanted to be free of him, he would let her go. Well, he would try. But in all honesty, he would give her anything she wanted, if he only knew she was okay.

If, in the end, she wanted him to go, he would. If that would make her happy, he would do it. Anything for her. Anything it took. He made a vow right then and there to do whatever she needed and wanted, just as soon as he knew she was safe.

A knock at the door had Michael whipping around, a snarl on his lips even as Hunter invited the person to come inside. He silenced his growling and tried to rein in the beast. Wasn't that difficult since the person standing there shocked the shit out of him. Michael would never have expected to see *her* waiting in the doorway with big, frightened eyes.

"Excuse me, Neta," the she-Tiger said and cast her gaze downward.

The scent of her fear had Michael's Tiger chuffing in response. He did not seem to care she was Pride and female, the beast just wanted his mate. the she-Cat hunched her shoulders and averted her gaze from all the males in the room.

Shit.

They were all on edge because of this, and they were scaring her. Michael nodded at Lance to cut off the sound of his growling, and the younger male did so immediately. He had not even been aware of it, or so his shamed face told Michael.

Pamela Brown had made great strides to make up for all that she had been a part of as a result of her association with Blake. Still, Michael did not believe it was her fault. The former Beta had used his position to cower those weaker than him, and to abuse the females of the Pride unbeknownst to the Neta. It was horrible, but she was not to blame.

"Yes, Ms. Brown?" Hunter asked.

"I, uh, I saw some of the men searching the apartment above Jessica's shop, and I heard what happened. After they left, I went in, and looked around myself, I figured maybe fresh eyes, anyway, um, I found this between the cracked floorboards on the staircase," Pamela explained and held up what looked like a plunger from a needle.

"What made you look after it had been searched, Pamela?" Hunter asked, curious.

"Well, your Honor Guard are all fine Tigers, Neta, but if someone did something bad, they wouldn't be, fine Tigers, or Shifters, or even just men. They would be scum and, *well*, I've been around scum. For whatever it's worth, Doctor, I hope she is alright," Pamela said to Michael.

"Thank you."

Michael took the plunger from her hand, and he sniffed it. Recoiling from the sharp, pungent stench of poison toxins and dark magic, he dropped it into the trash. His Tiger growled and his entire body vibrated with anger.

"That stinks! It's some kind of poison. Must have been made by a Witch or Shifter scientist. There are enough toxins in here to take down any adult Shifter!"

"What is in it?" asked Uncle Uzzi.

"*Aconitum, Yew, Hemlock, Nightshade,* and *Oleander* for starters. My guess is it's a potent blend of herbs and toxins that can severely incapacitate a Shifter. I also smell several members of the *Allium* family, along with *Methylxanthines.* For an exact ingredient list, I'd have to send it to the lab."

"Let's do that, but you know what this means?"

Hunter nodded, while Brayden carefully

extracted the plunger from the garbage and placed it in an envelope.

"One more thing---" Pamela interrupted. "There was a really distinct odor, but only in the farthest corner of the hallway. Like body odor and rotting garbage," she said, and her face was pinched in revulsion.

"Mikey," the Neta said, and Michael turned to face his leader, fur sprouted along his arms, and his fangs descended.

"She didn't leave," Michael announced with dead certainty. "Kylie was taken."

"But I don't understand. Why would you help Kylie?" Jessica asked Pamela, and Michael had to admit he'd been too far gone to question her motives.

"Look I know what you think of me, and believe me or don't, that's on you. I swear, I am telling the truth," Pamela said, shaking with anger and maybe some sadness. She turned to Michael, her face imploring him to trust her.

"Your mate was nice to my son, to Paulie---"

"You have a son?" Jessica gasped.

"Look, I just want to help," Pamela replied.

He noted the surprise in Jessica's eyes at discovering Pamela had a child. Michael knew, of course, having tended her during her pregnancy and Paulie's birth. Pamela had kept the boy to herself for whatever reason. It was none of Michael's affair. He simply did his job as the Healer. Hunter had been aware of the cub for the Pride records, but it was not either of their business whether she told anyone else.

"But Kylie doesn't even like you," Jessica pressed.

"Well, I've never given her a reason to like me. Look, even after what I did to Gretchen, she forgave me. Reg forgave me too. I know I have a lot to answer for, but I swear, I am doing my best. Kylie might not like who I used to be, but I am trying to change, for my sake and my son's. I just have to," she whispered the last.

"Thank you, Pamela." Hunter stood and placed his hand on her shoulder. "You are a valued member of our Pride. I should've taken better care of you and others like you. Please, forgive me."

The entire room seemed to still at the Neta's words, and even Jessica was moved to step forward. She took the other she-Tiger's hand and squeezed it.

"I second that," Jessica said. "Please, let me know what I can do to help the support group you and Gretch have started working on."

"I will, thanks, but I think we better look for Dr. Mikey's mate first," Pamela said, and raised her eyebrows, nodding to where he was standing with his back to the room.

Three-inch long, black claws tipped his fingers, and the fur that had begun to sprout along his chest and arms now covered his face. He felt his fangs elongate, protruding from his mouth as his chest heaved with unshed violence.

His mate was in trouble, and the Tiger inside of him was desperate to get her back.

"Mikey, do you know who took her?" asked Brayden.

"Yes. It was her old Pride," he growled. "The smell, Kylie hated that fucking smell. She'd described one of the rogue's stinking of garbage and being more than a little creepy. His name is Waylon Pitt and if he touched a hair on her head, I am going to rip his throat out," he said in a deeper, more gravelly voice than was typical, but that was his Tiger for you.

"Michael," Uncle Uzzi said and stepped forward. "Look at me and focus. You have to quiet your Tiger," he instructed, even as the half-shifted Tiger snarled in barely contained fury.

"Michael," the Witch insisted. "It is the only way to save her. You must push the animal down and focus on your *matebond*. Right now."

Michael blinked when the old man slapped him right on the nose. Foolish, cause the Cat wanted to take a good chunk out of the old Witch's digits, but he stopped himself and shook his head.

"Close your eyes, Michael. Search your soul. You must find the thread that is your matebond. You will know it when you see it."

Michael fell to his knees. He grunted, and growled, wrestling with his Tiger for supremacy until Uncle Uzzi's words sunk in. In order for him to find his mate, he needed his Tiger to be quiet. Once he understood that, the beast went from enraged to compliant.

"Good, now look for it, find the ethereal link between you and the one fated to be yours until the end of your days," he instructed in a cool and calm voice.

Michael did as he was told. He ferreted around that metaphysical plane where his beast rested when not called. Beneath the fog and mist, he searched until he found the silvery flowing thread that connected him to his one true and fated mate.

"Kylie," he growled, and opened his eyes. "I feel her, I can sense where they are heading."

"Enough to drive?"

"Yes, let's go---"

The door to Hunter's office slammed open. All heads turned and stared at the entryway. Uh oh. There stood one hugely swollen, huffing, and puffing, angry as fuck Elissa Maverick with Gretchen toting behind, an apologetic expression on her face.

The seriously peeved Nari took in each of the room's inhabitants in her angry blue glare before she opened her mouth and roared at the lot of them. More than one head turned down, and several pairs of eyes averted out of respect as she made her displeasure known. Once she was done posturing, the Alpha fem of the Maverick Pride stomped her feet and placed her hands on her belly to steady herself.

"Alright you fuckers, this is supposed to be *my* baby shower. I went outside waiting to be pampered and praised, and my beyotches were supposed to sing *Baby Love* to me while I entered the tent on the karaoke machine, damn it! But no one I wanted was there!"

"Love, I apologize, *oof-*"

Hunter sucked in air as his mate's fist landed

squarely in his stomach. His teal eyes glowed, and where a lesser man might have sunk to the floor, he sucked it up, and managed to gaze adoringly at her even as she scowled.

"Shut it, buddy. Thanks to you, I'm the size of a fucking water buffalo, and twice as mean," she growled, and the lucky bastard smiled at her.

In fact, the fucker must've had a death wish because he leaned forward and kissed her brow, beaming at the furious woman like only a man in love would be foolish enough to do.

That was why Hunter was the Neta. The SOB was the biggest, baddest, and best pussy of them all. Save for maybe Elissa herself. After going through the Puspa, she had certainly embraced her wild nature. Everyone was sure their offspring would be total badasses, ruling the Pride by the time they went to school.

"Well? Someone tell me what the fuck is going on here!" she demanded.

"You see, Nari---" Brayden began.

"It's just---" Jessica interrupted.

"Love, you should be resting---"

"Someone took Kylie," Michael said, ignoring the shocked looks and angry glare of his Neta and the others.

Elissa walked to Michael, her blue eyes huge and concerned. She touched his forearm, her other hand was on her stomach.

"What are you doing to get her back?"

"I was just about to leave," he told her, aware of Hunter's displeasure.

"Well, then," she said, snapping a glance at her mate, who immediately shut the fuck up. "We better get going."

"Baby, I don't think---"

"Good, Hunter. Don't think, *my love*, just get the van because I am going with my Pride's Healer to get his mate and my friend back," she stated with absolute calm that was even more frightening than when she yelled.

"Elissa," Hunter began.

"I am going, Hunter. The question is, are you coming or not?"

"You heard her," Hunter growled, snarling at Brayden, who held up the keys as he took his wife's hand and placed a fierce kiss to her palm.

"Let's go!"

Michael didn't wait to be told, he was already gone. His long legs ate up the length of the hallway to the side door in just a few strides. Once everyone was situated, Michael sat up front, riding shot gun while Brayden drove.

How he wound up inside one of those twelve seater vans the Pride had for long distance runs with his very pregnant Nari, his Neta, the Pride Beta and his mate, Reg, Gretchen, Lance, Pierce, Pamela, Uncle Uzzi, and the Witch's limo driver, Hank, he would never even try to understand.

"I know what you're thinking, Mikey," Elissa said. "You wanna know how come you got a van full of Pride coming to get your mate."

"How did you know that?"

"Cause all you men are the same," She said and grinned. "But you are forgetting one thing. Kylie may be your mate, but that she-Tiger is one of my best friends. Fuck that, she's family. I will always be there for my family," Elissa vowed, and the others in the van growled and roared in agreement.

Michael nodded, beyond touched by her words, and he could not wait to tell Kylie. She would just about burst knowing what the Nari said. After he got her back, he would tell her everything. Well, after he'd loved on her for a few days.

He growled softly in his throat. Closing his eyes, Michael focused on the steadily pulsing *matebond* that was acting as some sort of otherworldly GPS and leading him straight to where those soon-to-be-dead rogues who abducted his mate were taking her.

Luckily, the assholes only had a couple of hours' head start. With his pedal to the metal, and some knowledge of South Jersey's back roads through the Pine Barrens, and a very understanding Jersey Devil who had allowed them to use his family's land as a cut-through, Brayden soon had them dead to rights.

"She is close," he growled.

The sun had already set, but the feel of their matebond strengthened the closer Michael got to Kylie. Brayden pulled over at Michael's indication. A beat up truck was parked at a deserted rest stop off I-95.

The gas station was still active, but the restaurant and tiny convenience store had long since been closed. The fuckers parked way in back, so as not to be seen, he figured.

"Stay here," Michael growled as he exited the van.

They had parked on the other side of the lot where there was only one other car present.

Michael ignored it and walked towards the other battered old pickup. He could not see anyone inside, but the scent of flowers and spice was strong.

Kylie.

His heart squeezed in his chest. She had been

there, he was certain, but it appeared he was too late, he thought as he moved in closer.

Wait a second, he paused. Rubbing a hand over his face, he wanted to be sure he was not seeing things.

"Kylie!"

He noticed a prone shape lying down across the ripped and scarred seat. It was her inside that filthy vehicle. Michael ran without hesitation and grabbed the door handle.

He recognized her blonde hair and her unique scent, that was forever tinged with faint traces of his own mint essence. His beast gained satisfaction from that change in her fragrance, but anger quickly replaced that feeling at the state she was in.

She was slouched over, her breathing wheezy and troubled. Green eyes stared, tearing up as she struggled to blink.

"Hang on, kitten," Michael said as he opened the creaky door.

"Michael," she barely whispered, weak as she was.

Her breathing grew jerky, and he smelled her fear. That only made his Tiger more aggressive. Fury at the fuckers who stole her, he noted his hands shook as he attempted to sit her up and looked at her pupils.

He was going to kill those bastards, he vowed to himself. He did not like her afraid. Every instinct he had pushed him to get her out of that stinking vehicle and home where he could keep her safe and secure.

Michael's heart thundered as he bent over and placed one arm around her back and the other under her knees. He pulled her across the torn seats and growled at the discarded waste and stains that she'd been sitting on.

Those bastards were going to pay for this. It was not only an insult to his mate, but to him as a Tiger and a Healer as well. Whether she wanted him for keeps or not, she was his to avenge.

His.

Anyone who thought otherwise was welcome to find out for themselves just how fucking serious he was. The moment he moved to lift her out of the disgusting truck, Michael froze. The cold muzzle of what he expected was a rifle pressed against his ribs.

"What kind of Shifter brings a gun to a Cat fight?" he snarled the question.

Pussy, snarled his Tiger---the animal had clearly spent too much time with Uncle Uzzi.

"Easy there, fella," growled a young male, a Tiger

from the scent of him, but not of the Maverick Pride.

Michael already knew it was not one of his own that had dared kidnap a female, especially a claimed one. Still, he would not risk his sweet mate for all the world.

Hating what he had to do, he met her scared eyes and tried to impress upon her everything he was feeling. He placed her on the seat and turned slowly, hands raised.

"N-no," Kylie struggled to sit up.

"Easy," he told her, concern for her making him stupid.

The douche bag with the gun hit him hard in the ribs, and he grunted, but refused to fall. He needed to make sure Kylie was safe before he could even consider what was about to go down.

Her fast metabolism would normally burn through the toxins these animals injected her with, but the bastard who mixed the potion would account for that. Michael didn't necessarily think the two idiots who'd done this had the capacity to think that scientifically.

"Well, well, this here the boy who plucked your flower, girl?"

Another approached, and this man's accent was

harsh, his voice rough and cruel. Michael turned his head slightly away from the younger male who was holding the rifle to the older, bearded man whose stench was at once upon him, and most reviling. Hell, it was all he could do to keep from puking on the bastard.

"You might wonder why it is that a Shifter such as myself has such a profound and disturbing body odor," the soon-to-be-dead man walked around to Michael's front.

"You see, I was a bit of a heartbreaker in my youth and in my days of sowing wild oats, well I *kinda mighta* done wrong to a Witch I promised to mate. This was her revenge," he growled, lifting his arms, causing more putrid stench to fill Michael's sensitive nostrils.

"Ya learn to love it," the psycho said, barking a laugh that ended with a growl.

"I sincerely doubt that," he replied.

"Yeah, well, boy, I *sincerely* don't give a rat's ass. We gonna do this? I got a Pride to take," the man said.

He barely nodded when the younger Shifter pulled the trigger. Pain exploded in Michael's left shoulder, and he roared his fury while Waylon laughed and removed his shirt, but before he could launch himself at the wounded Healer, the rest of the Maverick Pride who'd accompanied him suddenly surrounded them.

"Hell, boy, you didn't have to bring no backup," Waylon snorted, then turned to address the rest of them.

"Lookee, here now, I'll take this to the Council if all y'all interfere in this here business! I already got them to listen to my claim. Now, y'all just stay there while I finish goody-two shoes off."

"STOP! You will stop these actions, Waylon Pitt," Hunter said, and stepped forward.

He exuded Alpha strength, commanding the obedience of all present. This was a true Neta, and the difference between him and Waylon was only too obvious.

"You have attacked two of my own. You have kidnapped the claimed mate of our Pride Healer after unlawfully entering my territory without permission with the intent to kidnap her. Since she is one of my Pride, that is an offense punishable by death," the Neta of the Maverick Pride growled.

He was menacing, with his bald head and rippling muscles. A huge mountain of a man, and one royally pissed off Tiger. He was almost as angry as Michael himself.

Almost.

First things first, though, Michael was all about his mate. Before he could mete out justice to the two infiltrators, he turned his back on Hunter and Waylon as they growled and traded insults and accusations. To be honest, he didn't give a fuck about the two Tigers' differences.

Kylie was his only concern. She was struggling to stand, and he could hear her pulse racing, trying to rid her body of the poison.

"No, no, save your strength," he said, and winced as his shoulder throbbed in time with his heartbeat as it bled.

It should have stopped by now, but for some reason it still flowed an angry red. Then it hit him, the bastards laced the wounds with toxins. Shit. That would slow him down.

He followed her horrified gaze and saw the stain slowly spreading, bleeding through his shirt.

"It's okay, these assholes poisoned the bullets and shot me, but it will wear off," he said.

Tears rolled down her face, but Kylie still did not speak. She couldn't. Michael's heart tore a hole inside of him.

Fuck.

Only the most dishonorable of Shifters would do

such a thing, but he did not want her to worry. He tried to brush it off. He took her chin in his hand and made her look at him.

"I am fine, Are you okay?" he asked as the men, one real Neta and one wannabe, continued to argue.

"Your Yankee claims are false! I am her real Neta. She is my Pride, and was promised to me by her mother," bellowed the man Michael was about to kill.

He turned and shielded Kylie with his body, growling at the asshole. His Tiger did not blink at the thought. Healers knew death. It was a part of life, and Michael was a Shifter. He was a hunter, a predator, a lethal killing machine and his honor, and his mate had been wounded.

Yes, he wanted the fucker dead.

The Healer in him valued life. That was the truth. But this foul-smelling piece of shit had threatened his mate. He had no qualms about what he was going to do.

"M-Michael---p-poison," she whispered, and he turned around to see her eyes fill with tears.

"I'm okay, you will be too, I swear it," he vowed.

"Help me," she asked, and he did, signaling the women over.

Jessica and Pamela rushed to flank her sides

and thank goodness, Gretchen held Elissa back. Hunter glanced at his mate first, then at the younger male still standing too close, holding the gun he'd shot him with. The Tiger yelped, dropping the weapon, and stood with his hands raised.

"You gonna drop that gun when your Neta is depending on you, boy," Waylon yelled at the man, whose eyes were now glued to the floor.

"You are no *Neta*. In fact, your pitiful attempt to steal the leadership of the Sharp Claw Pride has been reported to the Council. They have already sent an envoy to dispel your corrupt brethren and to ensure the safety of the rest of the Pride."

"But, but you can't do that," Waylon Pitt tugged his beard and spit on the ground.

"I have done that. Now you will answer to me for the misdeeds you have committed to my Pride. Michael Turner?"

He heard his name but needed to make sure Kylie was okay, kissing her once on the mouth and pressing his head to hers before facing his Neta. He forced himself to ignore her weakened whimper, adding it to the many reasons why he was going to nail this sonovabitch to the wall.

"Yes, Neta," he answered his Alpha.

"Do you wish to seek justice for the crimes against your mate?"

"I do."

"No, Michael, he's not worth it," said Kylie in a stronger voice than she'd previously produced.

"Kylie McNaughton-Turner, it is your mate's right to answer these crimes and as this person is claiming you belong to his Pride, it is the law. Either this gets met out today, or you could be forced by the Council to return to the Sharp Claw Pride until the details can be worked out." Hunter's voice was still laced with his power, but there was no mistaking the anger in his tone.

The Council could be such a bunch of shitheads.

Michael knew his Neta had been dealing with them when they'd been driving in the van, searching for his mate. He knew something drastic would have to be done.

"If I may have one moment, Neta, to say goodbye to my mate?"

"Better say goodbye, cub, I'll be spreading her thighs before the sun sets," Waylon grunted so only Michael could hear.

The rest of the Pride waited until Hunter nodded. They spread out, forming a circle as best they could in the graveled lot. They'd rounded the corner despite the angry mutterings of their Nari, who was adamant she did not want this to happen.

Mikey felt for her. After all, she was his patient and his Alpha fem. Pregnancy made even the most docile females hormonal at times. He did not like upsetting her, but nothing could stop him from defending his mate. He needed to end the threat, here and now.

They were far enough away from the road so as no passers-by could see. The noise from the gas station would help cover the sound of the fight. Luckily, it was run by a Gorilla Shifter and his family. Under the circumstances, secrecy was necessary.

Yes, Hunter could pass this off as a legitimate fight, but he might still get crap from the Council. They liked to stick their noses in after the fact.

"Michael, please, you have to understand, he is not honorable. You could get hurt," Kylie grabbed his shirt and pulled herself into a standing position out of the other two ladies' hands.

They turned their heads but lingered near in case she needed them. He was grateful for that, even for their pretending not to listen. Not like they could help it with their supernaturally enhanced hearing capabilities.

"*Mon petit chaton,*" he whispered to her in the French his grandmother had taught to him when he was just a boy.

"What's it mean?" she whispered.

"It means *my little kitten* and that, my love, you most definitely are. A tiny little thing, but a fierce she-Tiger all the same. And mine, Kylie. Most of all, you are mine."

"Michael, I don't want you hurt, just let me go with him and maybe the Council---"

"Never," he growled, teeth bursting from his gums, eyes wild. "Mine."

Kylie's face softened, and she ran her hands over his chest and shoulders, soothing his Tiger.

"I know, mate. I only meant let me talk to the Neta. I know I am yours, Michael. I want to be yours forever. And you are mine," she told him, clinging to him, and claiming his lips so sweetly he almost caved, but he knew he couldn't.

"I'll be okay," he said, pressing a kiss to her forehead. "I have to do this so you can be free. Leave or stay, you have to choose Kylie. It wasn't right for me to take away your choice. This is the only way I can give it back to you," Michael told her, gasping at the end.

His breathing was growing difficult as the poison

worked its way through his blood. The gunshot wound still bled, but this was his fight. He thought of all the possibilities, but he knew this was the only way he could give her the chance she deserved to choose her life for herself.

"I don't understand---" Kylie's celery green eyes questioned him, and he could see her struggling to recover from the drugs she'd been given.

"Someone, give her water! It will help her metabolize the toxins," he barked out the rough command.

"Kylie, know this, I love you so much, more than anything in the world."

"Then why set me free?"

"Baby, I never want you to leave me. Nothing could be farther from what I want, but I know I bullied my way into your life and that wasn't fair. I should've wooed you. Should've made you fall in love with me, the way I fell for you. Naturally. I shouldn't have just announced it in the middle of Hunter's office. I was an ass."

"Well, then you were my ass," she said, and her lower lip wobbled. "Please, don't fight him."

"I have to. The choice to stay with me needs to be yours. Fated or not. You will get to decide your future once I finish this. Just know that whatever you decide, I love you."

The poison was slowing down Michael's reflexes, but he had one thing Waylon didn't, and that was Kylie's best interest at heart.

She was his breath, his body, his very soul. Michael could not live without any of those, and he would never give her up to this piece of shit.

Grrrr.

Chapter Thirteen

I love you.

Those three words echoed in Kylie's mind for what seemed like an eternity, but in reality, was a mere moment.

The area behind the old diner and shifter run gas station was dusty and littered with debris and old boxes. She watched as some males, men of the Maverick Pride removed the offending items. Making the brutal pit they were creating cleaner, she supposed.

As if a dang milk crate mattered to two dueling Shifters! She sucked in a sharp breath, nearly passing out as she realized she had forgotten about the whole needing oxygen thing for a minute.

I love you.

He'd told her he loved her. Not for the first time, but it was the first time she had really heard him. At first, declarations of love seemed so easily mistaken for post-orgasmic euphoria. But this was not the time or place for that.

Michael had proclaimed his love after racing after her like her very own knight in shining armor, or in this case, an enormous van owned by the Maverick Pride. She could have laughed, but then again, not really.

The entire world seemed to slow as Michael left her embrace and headed towards the makeshift fighting pit. Kylie's heart thudded in her chest.

She'd seen this too many times. Had felt it for herself what it meant to be surrounded by eyes that could only watch as you fought for your life.

"I will tear your head off! Then we will all see if the *Healer* can heal himself," hissed Waylon as he removed his shirt and shoes and crouched down, running his claw-tipped hands along the gravel.

The stench from his body permeated the air and there wasn't a single Shifter there who didn't twitch his or her nose. That alone was like a bonus weapon or something. Had to be against the rules, she thought, and realized she was getting hysterical.

"I won't allow this." Elissa stomped her foot,

arguing with her mate with one ever present hand on her protruding belly.

The Nari was admittedly upset and scared for one of her own, and Kylie had never loved the other woman as much as she did just then. Who knew a former human could be such a good leader? Certainly not anyone in her old Pride.

She drank the icy water Jessica held to her lips and watched from where she stood as Michael removed his own shirt and shoes. His wound still bled freely, and he seemed to slouch. Worry gnawed at her gut.

They had agreed to start the fight as men, but all bets were off once they were in a full on battle-lust. Shifting mid-fight was allowed, though most deemed it cowardly.

"No," she whispered, as she watched Hunter walk to the middle of the circle.

"You all know our ways," the Neta began. "This man entered our territory and attempted to kidnap our Healer's mate, a crime that demands justice. The opponents will shake hands before the trial by combat begins."

The statement was met with growls and hisses from the small gathering, but Kylie ignored them all.

She was focused on Waylon. On that tiny smirk on the corner of his foul mouth.

Something was not right.

She watched as his hands played with the gravel. Lifting the loose, jagged rocks and dropping them again. Over and over. Biding his time. Like the spider who set the trap for the fly.

Kylie's eyes narrowed.

He was going to cheat. She knew it before Hunter waved his hand and her Michael, her sweet honorable Michael turned to shake Waylon's hand. The latter's smirk grew wide and as he pretended to offer his hand. Instead, he wheeled it back and hurled a fistful of tiny sharp rocks right into Michael's eyes.

Her mate roared in outrage and wiped at his face, only succeeding in digging the damn rocks further into his eyes. He was bleeding and growling, clutching his face. She knew he could do more damage if he tried to use his hands to clear the rocks.

"Waylon Pitt, you scumbag, you fucking cheated!" growled Brayden.

"I will have what I came for, Bear," he snarled, "and your Neta has given me the right to trial by combat, now will your Healer get up, and rise to the challenge or not? Maybe I should just take my prize and go," he sneered.

"He can't do that, can he?" Elissa asked, and she was perspiring in her anxiety.

"No one else can fight him or we risk having to stand trial with the Council. It's against our laws," Hunter growled.

"What? That can't be," she cried.

"Aghhh!" Michael was kneeling, and Brayden was attempting to clear his eyes with water.

"Just give me a minute," he growled, but she could tell he was in too much pain, and what's more, he was temporarily blinded by the injuries.

"If he can't fight me now, he forfeits, and I get Kylie," snarled Waylon, his overconfident grin as disgusting as his smell. "Those are the rules. After I kill him, I take the girl."

"No!" Kylie growled and stood up without Pamela's and Jessica's help.

It was not easy. Her body felt sluggish from the effects of the poison. She couldn't move as quickly or as confidently as she always had. Most disturbing of all was the fact that her she-Tiger seemed too quiet. The ever-present beast was a mere whisper in her mind's eye. But it didn't matter now, she had to do something.

Anything.

"Wait!" she said.

"Kylie, our laws are clear---" Hunter began.

"Yes, I know," she said, walking to the center of the circle. "Our laws are very clear, Neta. I claim the right to avenge mine and my mate's honor," she announced proudly, standing straight before them.

"What?"

"She can't!"

"Kylie!"

"No!"

Despite the cacophony of voices, her eyes narrowed in on Waylon's. She registered his surprise, followed quickly by a rage so intense she almost shied from it. Next, she turned to Hunter.

"Hunter, it is my right," she insisted.

"Kylie, are you sure?"

"No, you can't let her do this," Michael growled, and stumbled as he stood, his eyes ran with blood and Brayden held him back.

"Neta?" she asked again, ignoring her mate's anguished protests and the rest of her Pride.

God, she loved them so, and any one of them would do the same thing. It was that knowledge that kept her back ramrod straight. Kylie had been running too long. It was time she faced her past.

Even if it meant death. With one last look at Michael, who was shaking with rage and being held back by three of their own, Kylie took a fortifying breath.

"Okay," Hunter said, "begin."

Waylon came at her with the lazy confidence of a man who had no qualms about hitting women. She knew then that he'd been the one to kill her mother. It was obvious in the zeal he could not play off as something else, shining in his eyes, and the swagger in his stride that the creep did nothing to hide.

Kylie wished she could feel sorrow for her last living parent, but she did not. Nor did she hate him for killing her. There was no love lost between her and Corinne Connelly.

Kylie had a real family now. She had a mate, and she would do everything in her power to ensure no one would ever threaten either of them again.

"Y'all sure ya wanna do this, Kylie girl? You wanna take me on by yourself?" Waylon sneered at her, and she braced herself for the stench coming off him.

"I've never been more sure of anything, you foul-smelling sonovabitch," she growled.

With moves faster than any normal could ever comprehend, Waylon attacked. Slicing through the air, he hurled his clawed fists at her from every which way.

Kylie was sluggish and hurt from the drugs he'd given her, but she'd been raised by the most brutal Pride she'd ever encountered. Even slow, she was able to move out of his way to avoid being hit. He was bigger and stronger, that was true, but she'd always been quick.

Being petite was something she'd hated her whole life, but now she was grateful. Kylie flitted from one end of the circle to the other, waiting for Waylon to tire himself. She heard Michael speak her name and lost focus for a second, that caused her to receive a sharp scratch down her left arm. Still, she was able to avoid his grasp with a pivot and a tumble.

"Dammit, girl, stay still," he snapped.

As if.

Finally, she must've angered him to the point of no return with all her evasive techniques, because good ol' boy that he was, Waylon, the smelly fucker, shifted. Kylie vaulted over his still changing shape and using all her strength, she called on her she-Tiger.

"Holy fuck! She's shifting midair," someone---maybe Jessica, or was it Elissa---hissed in the crowd.

She couldn't say for sure, Kylie had to use all her focus on getting her she-Tiger' ass in gear. She had one shot at this and the stakes were too high for her to fuck this up. With a resounding roar, she landed on her opponent's back in her fur.

The massive Tiger could not dislodge her. He snarled and hissed, trying to reach around, but falling short of his mark. Kylie dug her claws into the fleshy bits of his neck, snarling loudly right before she pulled with all her might. The resounding crack of Waylon Pitt's neck breaking echoed in her ears before she heard the celebratory roar of her Pride filling the air.

Huffing and panting, she snarled one more time at the now dead, and still stinking Tiger before she jumped off him and ran over to where her mate was still being held back by his Pride mates. Michael was squinting at her, and his eyes and the surrounding flesh, though still torn and bloody, were already on the mend.

"Kylie," he said, practically exhaling her name.

He dropped to his knees and opened his arms wide. Without hesitation her she-Tiger moved forward, licking his face, and knocking him off his feet with her strength. She cleaned the blood off his face with the flat of her scratchy tongue, refusing to let up until laughter bubbled up inside his chest.

"I'm okay, *mon petit chaton*," he said, and pressed his forehead to her feline one.

Kylie purred against him. In this form, her she-Tiger was absolutely certain of her feelings for the male. He was her fated mate, and she loved him more than words could ever say.

"Scared me to death, kitten. Don't you ever do that again," he growled, and she felt his worry, and hurt through their ever stronger *matebond*. "Change back, let me make sure you are fine, mate."

Kylie didn't hesitate. She felt the familiar hum of magic fill her body until her very bones vibrated with it. Shifting could be painful if one fought it, but she'd been born to this. Kylie's shift was fluid, graceful. One breath she was an eight-hundred pound beast, and with the next she was her usual curvy self.

"Mate," she said, and allowed her male to embrace her, wrapping her in his shirt at the same time.

"Kylie," he breathed, and locked his lips with hers.

The kiss was deep, needed, and so damn arousing that she felt moisture pool between her legs. She wanted him right then, right there, but of course they had an audience. A tap on Kylie's shoulder reminded her of that teensy fact, and she brought her head up to see the pained blue eyes of her Nari.

"Hey girl," Elissa said, smiling through tears. "So, yeah, I am like super glad you two are all good, and everything, but I kinda need my Healer. Like RIGHT FUCKING NOW. AHHHHHHHHH!" Elissa Phoenix Maverick roared, clasping her belly as a rush of fluid flowed between her legs just before she collapsed onto her knees on the floor of the graveled parking lot.

A few things happened then, and all in rapid succession. Kylie and Michael both caught their Nari before any more of her fell to the ground. They helped her stand one on each side. Pamela tossed Kylie a pair of sweatpants and took her place by Elissa's side so she could pull them on to stop her mate's anxious growling.

Brayden took Waylon's limp body and tossed it into the back of his pickup truck, covering it with a tarp and some tree branches and leaves. He and Jessica placed Waylon's second, the young asshole who shot Michael, under arrest and drove the truck back to the Pride House, where he would wait until the Council arrived to take him into their custody.

"Hank! Bring the van here. Don't worry, Elissa, you are going to be just fine. Hunter, don't you pussy out on your wife now," the old Witch yelled. "Hold her hand, damn it, now move!" Uncle Uzzi called out instructions, and started shouting orders, which everyone was only too happy to follow.

After piling into the van, Hank took the wheel while anyone not involved with the immediate care of the Nari was in the back row. Hunter cradled Elissa's head on his lap, and they took over the first bench of the van.

"I need light!"

Michael squinted as he took the waistband of Elissa's pants in his hands. Hunter snarled at him, but Michael met his Neta's angry glare. He had work to do, dang it.

"Hunter, dammit, I need to see how far she's progressed," he snarled right back.

"For the love of Christ, move! I will undress her."

Kylie stepped forward and took the elastic pants from her mate's hands, calming their Neta at once.

"Really, Kylie, you ought to b-buy me dinner-r firrrssstt," Elissa's grunted reply soon turned to a groan, and she turned her head in Hunter's lap. "Hurts so much."

"I'm so sorry, love," Hunter whispered, looking scared to death as he cradled her head.

"How sorry? Like sorry enough to do something for me?"

"Anything," Hunter vowed.

"I want you to *SIIINGGG-OWWWWIE!*".

"Now? Sing now?" Hunter asked, like an idiot.

"Not now. On *Whine Wednesday*," she said, sucking air in and puffing it back out in rapid succession.

"It will be okay, Elissa. And yes, I am a witness, Hunter will sing for you on the next karaoke slam session. Right now, though, you just focus, and listen to Michael, okay? You are strong, and you can do this," encouraged Kylie.

"That's right, you were made for this Elissa," seconded Uncle Uzzi from the back.

Hank drove like the wind as Michael did his examination. It was difficult in the confines of the van, but they were back at the Pride House sooner than expected.

"Hank has his ways," Uncle Uzzi explained as the Alpha couple were ushered into the one operating room inside the Pride clinic.

"Will she be okay?"

Hunter's teal gaze froze Kylie in her tracks as she moved to get Michael some more light.

"Yes. Michael is an excellent Healer, and more

than qualified doctor. The Nari will be fine," she replied and looked her Neta dead in the face for longer than ever before.

She nodded encouragingly. After all, she spoke the truth. She had every faith in Michael's abilities as a Healer. Of course, she knew the stories. Shifter births were never easy on anyone. But she had to believe for all their sake's that things would go well.

The future of the Pride depended on it.

Chapter Fourteen

Michael worked with Elissa, whose laboring lasted for seven long hours. The delivery was rough since the baby was breached, and an even bigger surprise, was the fact baby number one was a twin.

"Two cubs!" the Neta shouted his joy.

Both delivered right after midnight, the entire Pride had turned out around the Pride House to celebrate.

"No wonder she'd craved all that food," Jessica whispered.

"Yeah, just in the last few days I saw her she ate like double the amount of protein I did when I was pregnant with Paulie," Pamela offered.

"And yet, no scan revealed that she was carrying

multiples," Brayden added, shaking his big Bearish head.

"They are so beautiful." Tears of joy rolled down the Neta's face as he held both little girls in his arms. Elissa drifted off, her body healing itself of the wear and tear of natural birth.

"They are," Kylie agreed, before Hunter bent down, dropping a kiss on his sleeping wife's brow.

"She did very well, Neta," Michael said and smiled as his nurse, who'd arrived late, took the cubs, and placed them in the bassinet next to the sleeping new mother.

"Thank you, Mikey, from the bottom of my heart," Hunter told his friend and Healer, before turning to sit closer to his mate.

Michael nodded to his nurse, then he and Kylie both left the room quietly. The air seemed charged with the turbulent emotions, and not just because of Michael and Kylie went through, but because of what they had all experienced together.

"You have my number in case of an emergency," Michael told the nurse, his hand possessively resting on his mate's arm.

"Of course, and I'll stay through the night. I just charged my tablet," she replied, waving the small device happily. "My plan is to read my favorite romance author's new series in between checking on our patients."

"Oooh, what's it about?" Kylie inquired.

"Oh, it's a hoot! This series is about these feisty witches and their Shifter mates!"

Marina waggled her eyebrows, and Kylie smiled, laughing with her as the woman followed the mated pair out of the room. She was a widow and part of the Pride. The she-Tiger was also a registered nurse and one of the best he had ever worked with. Went to sit behind her desk with her latest bounty of ebooks.

The woman could not seem to get enough of them, and Michael didn't mind if she read on the job as long as she got her work finished. Elissa's she-Tiger was already hard at work healing the Nari, and the young were doing well, so it should be a smooth night for all.

Michael was dead tired and wanted a shower, but more than that, he wanted to get Kylie home and alone. He had not been able to pay much attention to her after the cubs had been born. His chest tightened, and his pulse raced, squeezing her arm where he held it, Michael hurried them back to their home. At least, he hoped it was going to be theirs.

"Come on," she said, calming his amped up

nerves with her sultry voice.

Kylie led the way through the empty living room and kitchen, down the hallway to the master bedroom. His cock pulsed inside his pants, and he knew he should give her time to get over what had happened, but he could not stop wanting her.

She walked them both inside the enormous bathroom he'd recently refurbished with dark blue glass tile, accented with flecks of green the same color as her eyes. The effect was gorgeous, like they were standing in the Mediterranean when in reality they were in their own home.

She turned to face him, her face full of such heat, he almost tripped over his own feet. Kylie held his gaze as she turned on the faucet to the shower and stripped away her clothes.

Fucking hell.

She was so beautiful. Petite and perfect with dusky tipped breasts and pale skin, he could not stop touching. He loved the way her soft belly molded to his hard body, the gentle flare of her hips, and that superb peach of an ass he wanted to nibble on for a day or two.

Kylie had the kind of body built for loving, and he planned on loving her until the day he died. Maybe longer.

"You still have your clothes on," she whispered, breaking his concentration as she stepped backwards into the large shower stall.

Rivulets of water streamed down her body, caressing every nook and cranny. Countless glistening beads of water, like thousands of little diamond droplets, kissed her skin, making her sleek and shiny. Like his very own treasured jewel.

Michael didn't hesitate. He stripped off his clothing and walked forward. Naked, heart on the line, fully erect and aching, he stepped into the stream of warm water and joined his mate.

"Mine," Michael growled, feeling the truth of his words with every fiber of his being.

A soul-deep rumbling began in his stomach, spreading through his chest and finally spilling out of his mouth as he found her lips with his in the shower. Kylie was ready, waiting, willing, and she opened for him like a flower waiting for the sun.

Humbled and honored, he kissed, and kissed, and kissed her some more, not rushing what was going to be a spectacular reunion---already was as far as he was concerned. His Tiger was right there with him, the beast fully aware and paying close attention to every response and reaction from his mate.

Her pleasure was his only goal. Securing her

safety and her love, his every intention. Michael waited a beat, growling softly as Kylie broke their kiss, watching intently as his sexy little mate took soap and washed his body.

She knelt down on the tiled floor of the enormous shower stall and started with his feet. He murmured a protest, but she shushed him and continued her journey.

"Let me, please, Michael," she whispered, and he found he could not deny her a thing.

His love swelled as readily as his cock as Kylie massaged his skin with her soft, sudsy hands and rinsed his limbs with the warm water. It was all he could do not to reach out and touch her, but something held him still.

"You don't have to do this, *ma petite chaton*," he said when he saw what she was about to do.

"I want you," she replied easily enough, and he hissed as he watched her place her hands on his hips, eye level with his straining dick.

Holy motherfucking shit.

His innocent little mate was going to take him into her mouth, and Michael almost came just from the image it presented in his mind. His Tiger growled fiercely, loving that she would do this, that she would trust him in this way.

Fingers running through her hair, he found her pink highlight she'd added to her golden locks, and he smiled. There it was her hidden wild streak. And it was just another of the many surprises he loved about her.

Michael braced himself as, with her celery green eyes glued to his, his beautiful little kitten leaned her blonde head forward and took the tip of his cock between her plump pink lips. She kissed the head and moved down the length of his shaft. Caressing his balls with her mouth before returning to wrap those lips around the tip once more.

Michael groaned as Kylie grew bolder, licking the slit and swallowing the little pearl of precum that dotted his mushroomed head. He hissed, grabbing her head gently with one hand, holding her steady, he rocked his hips and started fucking her mouth.

"S'good," he growled, trying to remain controlled, but she was quickly undoing his reserve.

He could not believe he was lucky enough to have an innocent as his mate, to be the first male blessed to initiate her into the carnal side of pleasure, but fuck, Michael was grateful. He would always treat her as she deserved, with the utmost care, respect, and love.

"Fuck," he moaned as she deep throated him,

making his eyes cross.

Kylie opened her sweet mouth wider, moaning as she took him down, the sound almost enough to make him come. His shaft emerged once more as she bobbed her head, sliding back and forth in an unhurried pace. Wet with her spit, he pulsed and throbbed under her innocently expert care.

Fuck, she was amazing.

Michael wanted to hang his head back and just enjoy, but he couldn't stop watching her. Her mouth felt fucking magnificent and the flat of her tongue was incredible. Most women did not like this sort of thing, but she seemed to.

As she moaned, she reached a hand between her legs and rubbed herself, all the while she continued to suck and fondle him with both her mouth and free hand.

Fuck, the sexy female was touching herself while sucking his dick, and he knew beyond a doubt. He was gonna come.

The water ran over him, warming his already heated flesh. Michael used one hand to steady himself on the shower wall and the other was still loosely wrapped around her neck and head. She covered his hand with hers, forcing him to close his tighter around her head.

"Mmm," she groaned.

Grrrprrrr.

Michael tried to be gentle, but his Tiger was fucking purring with pleasure. His little kitten wasn't having any of his reticence to come inside her heavenly mouth. She kneaded his balls and sucked him down hard. Moving her head and tongue faster and faster, fucking him with her mouth.

He shuddered as his orgasm washed over him, trying to remove himself from her mouth, but she stubbornly refused. Fucking woman was gonna suck him dry! And that only had him coming all the harder. Michael roared as he spilled his seed down her throat.

"Kylie," he growled her name as she swallowed until finally she released him.

Slowly, she moved her head until only her pink lips were kissing the tip of his spent cock. She lapped at the slit, cleaning him, and dazzling his senses at the same time before she stood to meet him, smiling like the cat that got the canary.

"Mine," she purred and mashed her lips to his.

Tasting himself on her tongue, Michael swept her off her feet in a fierce embrace and walked carefully out of the tub with her in his arms. He grabbed a fluffy towel and threw it over her body before heading to the bedroom.

"Kylie, Kylie, Kylie," he moaned her name, a litany on his lips before she reached up and locked her mouth onto his.

She was a beautiful temptation. One he wouldn't even bother trying to resist. Her spicy wildflower musk filled him, mixed with his own minty essence, and it penetrated his senses.

How he loved that scent. It was so uniquely theirs, and he couldn't wait to rub it all over himself.

"Mate," she whispered before tangling her tongue with his once more.

The sensation of kissing Kylie while having her damp, heated skin pressed against his had Michael's cock hardening instantaneously. His tongue dueled with hers for supremacy, and he was happy to let her win. Hell, he wanted her more than ever.

"I choose you, mate. Always you, Michael. Only you," she said, answering his unspoken question, and he thanked fuck for it.

"Mate," he said, pressing her back into the mattress before feasting on her bounty.

She was even more potent flat on her back with his tongue filling her slick channel. Without preamble, he'd dropped to his knees and splayed her legs wide. He ran the flat of his hand down her body to her slick pussy, spreading her lips and impaling her with his tongue. In and out, he thrust the long muscle, using his thumb to strum her clit while his other hand teased the crack of her ass.

"Michael, can't, fuck I can't," she shouted as another orgasm crashed over her.

The female writhed beneath his sensual assault, but Michael was so not letting up. He wanted more, demanded it. Tasting her salty sweetness, kneading the plump little nubbin between his fingers, Michael continued to fuck her mercilessly with his tongue.

"Did it feel like this when you were touching yourself, kitten? Did you come when you were sucking my dick?" he said while he strummed the needy little button.

"Oh fuck, mate, need you," she arched her back and lifted her hips, trying to force his mouth back on her.

He grinned wickedly and pressed her down with his hands, giving her only the whisper of his kiss on her most sensitive flesh. He wasn't sure how much longer he could hold out this time.

His cock was begging to fill her, the Tiger too. His beast clawed and chuffed, Demanding he take his mate. Yes, he needed to be inside of her.

Soon.

"Wanna be in you, kitten. Wanna fill you with my cum. Gonna mark you with my bite and my scent. Make you scream my name," he purred the words, meaning every one down to his very marrow.

"Yes, please," she begged.

That was all it took. Without any warning he opened his mouth and sucked that small bundle of nerves until she loosed a deep, guttural roar of a moan.

Then he took himself in his hands and pumped once, twice, enjoying the ripples of anticipation as they washed through him before placing his broad head at her slick entrance.

Her swollen pussy lips were pink and glistening in the moonlight streaming from the curtain-less window. She was fucking perfect. Beautiful, he thought as he rubbed her soft folds with his cock.

Michael took her legs and placed them on his shoulders. He tweaked her nipples and ran his hands down her soft belly to the gorgeous flare of her hips. His mate was all woman, and he loved every single inch of her.

"It's time you knew, you're mine," he pressed in two inches---"and I am never," ---another inch, "ever," ---one more, "ever," --- another, "gonna," ---

and another, "let," ---more still, "go," ---finally, Michael seated himself deep inside her hot pussy.

He thrusted his hips until every last inch of his steel length was buried happily inside his sexy little kitten. Fuck, he could die just like that, buried to the hilt in her hot, sweet, and undoubtedly wet pussy.

"Mine!"

Michael withdrew his cock, sliding almost completely out of her molten heat, before slamming back in. Again, he filled her in the same manner. And continued on that same path.

Long, hard, punishing thrusts that rocked the entire bed, and *hell*, the whole fucking house for all he knew. The sound of metal bending and wood snapping reached his ears, but he did not slow his pace.

The way Kylie's pussy squeezed him tight, milking his cock for everything he had, was more than worth it. Michael would buy another bed. Hell, he'd invest in more insulation.

Later.

Right then, he wanted to concentrate on her alone. He loved the feeling of her pussy squeezing his cock, coating him in her heady juices as he rocked her body into the same bliss he was feeling. Kylie was so fucking perfect, and their mating was meant to be. He knew it with every single bit of himself.

"I love you, Kylie," he growled. "My mate. Mine, mine, mine. MINE!"

"Yours, yes, yours!" Kylie moaned, a deep and guttural sound. Her claws raked down his back, scoring his skin.

The Tiger inside him growled, loving the way she marked him again for all to see. His fangs lengthened as he pounded into her. Her sheath stretched and squeezed as he filled her with his impossibly hard cock, stretching her to the max. The vibrato of their lovemaking echoed in the room. Michael couldn't get enough.

Her body was heaven. Soft and deceptively strong, she'd killed a man tonight with her claws. A threat to them both, and he loved her for it.

His Tiger scoffed at the idea that he could ever be jealous. All he felt for her was undying love and devotion. And if he could spend the next lifetime or two showing her, well, that would be enough for him.

"More," she growled, and he gave it to her.

Latching onto her breast with his mouth, he tugged on her nipple in time with the thrusting force of his hips. The combination proved to be just what his little mate needed, and as he felt his own orgasm rise as her pussy clenched. Finally, she screamed his name, as he promised she would.

"Michael!" she roared, and he struck, biting the side of her breast, and giving her another mating mark in the process.

The feeling of her own teeth clamping down on his neck had his dick bursting inside of her. Painting her uterus with his cum. Michael roared his completion, the sound rising above all others, filling his ears and the very air with his possessive victory.

Together, they collapsed on the mattress, clinging to one another until they could finally breathe once more.

"I love you," Kylie said in a voice that was soft as a butterfly's wings.

"I love you too," he returned her whispered vow, and he knew her she-Tiger understood.

Their matebond pulsed, and together they drifted off for a short nap. It would be many, *many* hours before either of them saw real sleep, engaged as they were in reclaiming and resealing their commitment and bond to one another.

"Mine," he purred against her mouth.

"And you are mine," she returned, and Michael had never felt so fucking good in all his life.

Chapter Fifteen

Kylie's she-Tiger ran in front of Michael's as they circled the woods behind *Jessica's Closet*. They had an hour before their first meeting of the *Maverick Pride Support Group*, led by Gretchen and Reg Cray and Pamela Brown.

Their three Pride mates had taken a lot of their own personal time to make this thing happen, and the least Michael and Kylie could do was to attend and support them. But first, she'd needed to stretch her legs and run in her fur.

Being mated certainly agreed with her, she thought with a pleasant chuff as she outran her mate. While she couldn't tell if he let her get away with it or not, one thing she knew was he was no slouch.

Not in any department.

After moving in with him, she soon realized Pride Healers had the worst working hours ever. As a designer, she pretty much set her own schedule, but no one could tell someone else when to be sick.

Thankfully, Kylie was largely able to adjust to his schedule so the pair could have the maximum time together. And when she needed to work, when her creative muses started bugging her to sit down and make something new, he was more than supportive and understanding.

Hell, he'd even encouraged her to take the business courses she'd been thinking about after he saw her browsing through a course pamphlet from the local Community College. As a successful entrepreneur, she really wanted to know more about business, and as a good mate, Michael was only ever helpful.

That didn't stop her from being ridiculously proud of her doctor mate. He took care of the entire Pride practically single handedly. Marina, their local RN, was a wonder, but she couldn't do everything he could.

From treating a usual case of the sniffles, to a cub who'd gotten his tail caught in a door, to delivering a set of twins and another single cub this month alone.

No matter what was up, the Pride laid it at their front door, and her mate did his best to tend all their needs, which actually made her love him all the more.

Michael nudged her side with his forehead and looked at her inquisitively. She realized she'd been stopped for some time. Chuffing in response, she padded over to a nearby stream and lapped at the cool water before heading back to the store and her old apartment to change.

Thankfully, Jessica had let her convert it to a workspace which the redhead had been happy to rent out to Kylie with the understanding that if Kylie made something, Jessica had first dibs at selling it. The she-Tiger was more than happy with the arrangement.

After changing back to their human skins, and the following smexy time shenanigans, the two got dressed. Michael turned and tugged Kylie closer until she was cradled in the safety of his arms. She couldn't get enough of that splendid feeling she got whenever he touched her, Sighing, she snuggled into his muscled chest.

It was the feeling of finally coming home.

"Did I ever say thank you?" he asked.

"For what?"

"For saving my life. For saving us," he answered.

She leaned back while still in his arms and held his sinfully sexy dark eyes in her gaze. How could she tell him everything she'd felt that day? Should she explain? In the end, she decided she wanted him to know.

"You don't have to thank me," she started. "Truth is, I was so angry at you for trying to be honorable, and setting me free, I think my she-Tiger burned through the toxins just so she could kick your ass," Kylie explained, and snorted at his raised eyebrows.

She was so incensed, Kylie didn't even bother trying to stop her Southern drawl from creeping in.

"I couldn't believe you said all that. I was furious, and I knew you were too good to go against a creep like Waylon. That man was a skunk, and he smelled like one too! I knew he'd cheat, and you would have never expected it because you were too good, too kind, and you value life in a way that wretched man could never have understood. I had to do something."

"So, you stepped up to save me, huh?"

He looked down at her, eyes glowing amber with his beast, and Kylie felt her pulse speed up. The handsome Tiger got her every time with his ridiculously sexy good looks.

"That's right, and I would do it again. Every single time," she leaned up on her tiptoes, but he held his head out of reach.

"Kylie, I love you like crazy, but let's agree that if there is a next time, it'll be my turn to do the saving. I could not bear to see you in danger, *ma petite chaton*," he growled and caught her mouth with his.

Warmth filled her and Kylie poured everything she had into that kiss. The fact he wanted to protect her was thrilling, but she was careful not to make any such promise. Honesty was the core of any relationship, but this was not something that was up for argument.

She would do everything she'd done a million times over. She would do anything for him, and she tried to let him know with her kiss.

All her love, her desire, her hopes and dreams, and every single ounce of trust and faith she had left was for Michael. She'd never have believed that a girl like the one she'd been could ever grow up to have a man like him.

"I love you, *mon petit chaton*," he whispered, and she savored the words from his lips.

His little kitten, her Tiger wanted to be insulted, but she secretly liked the nickname.

She didn't mind being called that, as long as

Michael was the one saying it. He was everything she needed and more. Looked like the doctor had finally caught her, and even more shocking, it was exactly where Kylie wanted to be. She wanted to be his mate.

She had expected conceit and arrogance from so handsome and educated a man, but what she got was patience and unwavering devotion. She'd expected him to shrink away from her strength and, okay, her beast's violent streak when it came to protecting him, and her new life, but he didn't.

In fact, no one had teased or sought to humiliate the Pride Healer for having a tougher than nails mate. She was pretty sure he'd gotten a few high fives after the whole thing had gone down. Kylie had to admit, it felt pretty darn good breaking that bastard Waylon's neck.

"When did they pick up that cub who was working with Waylon?" she asked her mate, knowing the young male had been gone that very morning.

"Ah, I see you've heard," he said. "Dakota Miles, the representative sent by the Council of Shifters, came at dawn to take him away. He led the envoy that liberated the Sharp Claw Pride from under the streak's rule."

"Good," she replied and sighed, glad to be done with it all.

"Actually, kitten, he had a question for you, and I've been waiting to ask."

"What is it?"

"Well," he said, and she ran a finger over the fine worry line between his thick dark brows. "He wanted to know if you were interested in ruling as Nari of the Sharp Claw Pride."

"What?" Kylie swallowed, having never really considered the possibility.

"Well, it wasn't just luck that had you fighting off the powerful concoction he'd poisoned you with or an accident that your she-Tiger was able to break his neck. You come from a long line of Alpha fems, Kylie McNaughton. Your Tiger is fierce and dominant."

She turned away from him and walked the length of the room. All her life she was made to feel small, told she was worthless and only meant to serve at her mother's feet. The only time she had ever felt like anything was here, in Maverick Point.

She didn't need time to think. It was a no brainer.

"Well?" he asked, and she could feel his anxiety lacing the air with a lemony tartness that made her she-Tiger' nose itch.

Kylie sneezed.

"Bless you," he said, and walked over, handing her a tissue.

"I'm fine," she replied, laughing, tucking her loose hair behind her ear.

"Michael, I don't want to be Nari. I don't want to return to the Sharp Claw Pride, or to rule over anybody. I just want to stay here with you."

"I would go with you, if that is what you wanted," he said, and she knew he meant it.

He would leave his home, career, family, and Pride for her. The sacrifice would be extreme, but he'd do it. She didn't doubt that for a second.

"I know, but I mean it. I don't want to leave Maverick Point. I love it here, and I love you."

"Okay then." Michael smiled, and it was like the sun coming out. He tucked her unruly locks back behind her ear and kissed her lips, pressing his forehead to hers.

"Mate."

"Mmm. Thank you, Michael, for everything. We should go," she murmured and took his hand and they walked to the meeting.

"Yep," he agreed.

"Well, looks like you caught me after all."

"Who me? In case you haven't noticed, kitten, I'm the one who's caught. Hook, line, and sinker."

"Good, I wouldn't have you any other way, Doc."

Kylie purred, pinching his ass, and laughing at his high-pitched yelp before walking into the room and taking a seat in the circle of chairs Reg had set up.

Looking around the room, she felt the pain and confusion of the Shifters who'd gathered. Shifters, mostly female, who'd been hurt by Blake and his men and their false ideology.

But there was one more thing she felt, something small and elusive, and it warmed her to the core, and that was hope.

Maverick Pride was truly a remarkable community, and Kylie knew she'd made the right choice to be a part of it and to stay with her mate. Michael sat close to her, his thigh brushed hers and he took her hand as the meeting started.

Yes, this was right where she belonged.

Epilogue

"For the love of farts!"

Elissa Maverick growled playfully as baby Melly flung a spoonful of mashed peas at her while little Celia added some butternut squash to the mix.

"What is going on in here?"

Kylie came running into the Pride House kitchen to see Armageddon, baby food style, taking place.

"Organic food has a calming quality, *my round ass*," growled the Nari.

Jessica joined the two women, and all three broke out in giggles as the twin girls continued to wage war against their mama for feeding them mashed veggies.

"They're Tiger cubs, Liss, you know they want meat," Jessica told her sister-in-law.

"I know that, but vegetables are a necessity. Her mate said so," the Nari returned and pointed at Kylie, who smartly raised her hands in surrender.

It still surprised her when someone mentioned her mate. True, she'd been mated a few months now, but as one half of a new couple, she was tickled by the moniker.

"Where is Doc Mikey, anyway?" Jess asked.

"He hates that name," she reminded them, and the redhead rolled her eyes and patted her swollen stomach.

Pregnancy was erupting all over the place within the Pride. With Gretchen two months behind Jess, and Kylie about to make her own announcement, they were sure to be overrun by diapers and wipes any second, which reminded her---

"So ladies, you know how I just got *KingZon* to let me have my own web store on their site and *Kisses by Kylie* has really taken off?"

At their nods she continued, "Well, check this out, *Mommies by Kylie* is now open for business, and I have added a collection of cloth diapers to the listings!"

The two women grabbed the brochures she'd had printed and seemed just as happy as she was with the results. After all, everyone had to do their part for the environment, so why not be pretty while you do it?

She helped wipe the twin girls clean and cuddled the chubby little cherubs while Elissa grabbed a platter of cold cuts for the women to share.

Jessica held Celia, who was as redheaded as her aunt, and Kylie held little Melly, who had hair black as a raven's wing. Both cubs had the teal eyes of their sire and were bound to be total heartbreakers.

Kylie sighed contentedly as she lay the sleeping Melly next to her sister in the playpen, then went to join the rest of the women who'd arrived for their weekly luncheon at the table.

Wine Wednesdays had indeed turned into *Whine Wednesdays*, this time baby soft whining was the reason for the moniker. The karaoke machine had been put away in favor of mobiles and soothing oceanic sound machines.

"Well, how is everyone?" their guest of honor, the infamous Uncle Uzzi asked, smiling as he looked around the room.

Kylie noticed when his blue gaze stopped with laser-like focus on the newest addition of their group. Pamela Brown was smoothing a hand over her newly shortened and silky, dark curls while Elissa filled her plate with pieces of fresh slices of prosciutto and cantaloupe.

"You need fattening up," the Nari insisted, and Pamela laughed.

The she-Tiger had put on a little more weight recently, and it was very becoming if Kylie did say so herself. She'd managed to turn her life around after their former Beta and the degenerates he'd been in bed with had very nearly destroyed her life.

Nowadays, they all welcomed the woman who had once tried to make Kylie's good friend Gretchen's life hell. It was all water under the bridge now.

"Pamela, dear, how are you?" asked Uncle Uzzi.

Elissa, Jessica, Gretchen, and Kylie looked at one another, then at Pamela, Uncle Uzzi, and back again.

"Uh, I'm good?" the she-Cat said, but it came out more like a question as she looked at the silent and staring faces of the women of the Pride.

"Really? Tell me, how would you like to have the best sex of your life?"

"What?" she sputtered, having just taken a bite of cantaloupe.

"Oh, I'm not offering for myself, dear. I am, as

you know, still happily married to my own darling wife, Gods rest her soul, but I have a feeling I have just the man for you," the famous matchmaker told the now shocked female.

"Oh, I don't want---"

"Have a cookie, sweetie," Elissa interrupted, and shoved a chocolate chip cookie into Pam's mouth.

"You might as well just give in. Uncle Uzzi always gets his way," Jessica added.

"But---"

"Shhh. Don't talk with your mouth full," Elissa said.

"If Uncle Uzzi has someone in mind, it really will be the best sex of your life," Gretchen added.

"You guys---"

"Amen to that!" Kylie drawled.

"If it wasn't for Uncle Uzzi, I'd never have caught my purrfect mate," she said aloud, winking as the man in question strode into the room.

"Hello ladies, Uncle Uzzi," Michael said and nodded.

He walked to where his mate sat, one hand immediately covered her stomach while the other held her face as he delivered one of his patented breath-stealing kisses to her waiting lips.

"How is *mon petit chaton* today?"

"*Bien*," she replied and kissed him back to a series of catcalls and wolf whistles.

But nothing penetrated the bubble that seemed to surround them whenever she was in Michael's arms. In the background, she heard conversation resume, and poor Pamela was being treated to an interview by Uncle Uzzi in front of the very loveable and unbearably nosy females of the Maverick Pride.

Poor thing, thought Kylie. *She doesn't stand a chance.*

"Let's go home." Kylie turned to her mate and nuzzled his nose with hers.

"Yes, ma'am," he answered, and she smiled radiantly at him.

Her heart swelled with love until she was near to bursting with it. No matter what happened in the future, there was one thing Kylie knew for sure. She was exactly where she belonged.

The Maverick Pride was her community and Maverick Point her address, but Michael Turner was her home now.

Always.

.   .   .

The end.

Did you enjoy this story? Check out the rest of the Maverick Pride Tales today! And look for the new edition of Shake That Sass coming soon!

P.S

Don't forget to tell me how you liked this story by leaving your honest review!

No pressure. 😉

A review can be one or two brief sentences where you simply state whether you enjoyed the story and would recommend it to someone! It is an enormous help to authors and the best way for us to reach larger audiences so we can keep writing the stories you love!

Thank you so much!

Xoxo!

Del mare alla stella,

C.D. Gorri

Beware... Here Be Dragons!

The Falk Clan Tales began as my stories surrounding four dragon Brothers and how they find their one true mates, but when a long lost brother arrives on the scene, followed by a few more Shifters…what can I say? The more the merrier!

Each Dragon's chest is marked with his rose, the magical link to his heart and his magic. They each have a matching gemstone to go with it.

She's given up on love, but he's just begun.

In *The Dragon's Valentine* we meet the eldest Falk brother, Callius. He is on a mission to find a Castle and his one true mate, one he can trust with his diamond rose....

His heart is frozen; can she change his mind about love?

In *The Dragon's Christmas Gift* our attention shifts to Alexsander, the youngest brother of the four. He has resigned himself to a life alone, until he meets *her*.

Some wounds run deep, can a Dragon's heart be unbroken?

The Dragon's Heart is the story of Edric Falk who has vowed never to love again, but that changes when he meets his feisty mate, Joselyn Curacao.

She just wants a little fun, he's looking for a lifetime.

We finally meet Nikolai Falk and his sexy Shifter mate in *The Dragon's Secret*.

Now available in a boxed set.

Guess what…. I've got more Dragons on the way!

Look for The Dragon's Treasure now available, and the upcoming The Dragon's Dream and The Dragon's Surprise!

Other Titles by C.D. Gorri

Young Adult Urban Fantasy Books:

Wolf Moon: A Grazi Kelly Novel Book 1

Hunter Moon: A Grazi Kelly Novel Book 2

Rebel Moon: A Grazi Kelly Novel Book 3

Winter Moon: A Grazi Kelly Novel Book 4

Chasing The Moon: A Grazi Kelly Short 5

Blood Moon: A Grazi Kelly Novel 6

*Get all 6 books NOW AVAILABLE IN A BOXED SET:

The Complete Grazi Kelly Novel Series

Casting Magic: The Angela Tanner Files 1

Keeping Magic: The Angela Tanner Files 2

G'Witches Magical Mysteries Series

Co-written with P. Mattern

G'Witches

G'Witches 2: The Hary Harbinger

G'Witches 3: Summoning Spells

<u>Paranormal Romance Books:</u>

<u>Macconwood Pack Novel Series:</u>

Charley's Christmas Wolf: A Macconwood Pack Novel 1

Cat's Howl: A Macconwood Pack Novel 2

Code Wolf: A Macconwood Pack Novel 3

The Witch and The Werewolf: A Macconwood Pack Novel 4

To Claim a Wolf: A Macconwood Pack Novel 5

Conall's Mate: A Macconwood Pack Novel 6

Her Solstice Wolf: A Macconwood Pack Novel 7

Werewolf Fever: A Macconwood Pack Novel 8

Also available in 2 boxed sets:

The Macconwood Pack Volume 1

The Macconwood Pack Volume 2

<u>Macconwood Pack Tales Series:</u>

Wolf Bride: The Story of Ailis and Eoghan A Macconwood Pack Tale 1

Summer Bite: A Macconwood Pack Tale 2

His Winter Mate: A Macconwood Pack Tale 3

Snow Angel: A Macconwood Pack Tale 4

Charley's Baby Surprise: A Macconwood Pack Tale 5

Home for the Howlidays: A Macconwood Pack Tale 6

A Silver Wedding: A Macconwood Pack Tale 7

Mine Furever: A Macconwood Pack Tale 8

A Furry Little Christmas: A Macconwood Pack Tale 9

Also available in two boxed sets:

The Macconwood Pack Tales Volume 1

Shifters Furever: The Macconwood Pack Tales Volume 2

The Falk Clan Tales:

The Dragon's Valentine: A Falk Clan Novel 1

The Dragon's Christmas Gift: A Falk Clan Novel 2

The Dragon's Heart: A Falk Clan Novel 3

The Dragon's Secret: A Falk Clan Novel 4

The Dragon's Treasure: A Falk Clan Novel 5

Dragon Mates: The Falk Clan Series Boxed Set Books 1-4

The Bear Claw Tales:

Bearly Breathing: A Bear Claw Tale 1

Bearly There: A Bear Claw Tale 2

Bearly Tamed: A Bear Claw Tale 3

Bearly Mated: A Bear Claw Tale 4

Also available in a boxed set:

The Complete Bear Claw Tales (Books 1-4)

The Barvale Clan Tales:

Polar Opposites: The Barvale Clan Tales 1

Polar Outbreak: The Barvale Clan Tales 2

Polar Compound: A Barvale Clan Tale 3

Polar Curve: A Barvale Clan Tale 4

Also available in a boxed set:

The Barvale Clan Tales (Books 1-4)

<u>Barvale Holiday Tales:</u>

A Bear For Christmas

Hers To Bear

Thank You Beary Much

Also available in a boxed set:

The Barvale Holiday Tales (Books 1-3)

<u>Purely Paranormal Romance Books:</u>

Marked by the Devil: Purely Paranormal Romance Books

Mated to the Dragon King: Purely Paranormal Romance Books

Claimed by the Demon: Purely Paranormal Romance Books

Christmas with a Devil, a Dragon King, & a Demon: Purely Paranormal Romance Books

Vampire Lover: Purely Paranormal Romance Books

Grizzly Lover: Purely Paranormal Romance Books

Elvish Lover: Purely Paranormal Romance Books

Christmas With Her Chupacabra: Purely Paranormal Romance Books

The Wardens of Terra:

Bound by Air: The Wardens of Terra Book 1

Star Kissed: A Wardens of Terra Short

Waterlocked: The Wardens of Terra Book 2

Moon Kissed: A Wardens of Terra Short

*Now in a boxed set and in audio!

The Maverick Pride Tales:

Purrfectly Mated

Purrfectly Kissed

Purrfectly Trapped

Perfectly Caught

& More coming

Dire Wolf Mates:

Shake That Sass

Breaking Sass

Pinch of Sass

Kickin' Sass (formerly Hot Dire Wolf Nights)

Wyvern Protection Unit:

SERIES MAKEOVER COMING SOON

Standalones:

The Enforcer

Blood Song: A Sanguinem Council Book

<u>EveL Worlds:</u>

Chinchilla and the Devil: A FUCN'A Book

Sammi and the Jersey Bull: A FUCN'A Book

Mouse and the Ball: A FUCN'A Book

<u>The Guardians of Chaos:</u>

Wolf Shield: Guardians of Chaos Book1

Dragon Shield: Guardians of Chaos Book 2

Stallion Shield: Guardians of Chaos Book 3

Panther Shield: Guardians of Chaos 4

Witch Shield: Guardians of Chaos 5

<u>Howl's Romance</u>

Mated to the Werewolf Next Door: A Howl's Romance

The Tiger King's Christmas Bride

Claiming His Virgin Mate: Howls Romance

<u>Twice Mated Tales</u>

Doubly Claimed

Doubly Bound

Doubly Tied

<u>Hearts of Stone Series</u>

Shifter Mountain: Hearts of Stone 1

Shifter City: Hearts of Stone 2

Shifter Village: Hearts of Stone 3

Accidentally Undead Series

Fangs For Nothin'

Moongate Island Tales

Moongate Island Mate

Mated in Hope Falls

Mated by Moonlight

Speed Dating with the Denizens of the Underworld

Ash: Speed Dating with the Denizens of Underworld

Arachne: Speed Dating with the Denizens of Underworld

Hungry Fur Love

Hungry Like Her Wolf: Magic and Mayhem Universe

Hungry For Her Bear: Magic and Mayhem Universe

Shifters Unleashed Boxed Sets

Check out these amazing anthologies where you can find some of my books and the works of other awesome authors!

Midnight Magic Anthology (Water Witch)

Rituals & Runes Anthology (Air Witch)

Island Stripe Pride

Tiger Claimed

Tiger Denied

<u>NYC Shifter Tales</u>

Cuff Linked

Sealed Fate

<u>A Howlin' Good Fairytale Retelling</u>

Sweet As Candy (as seen in Once Upon An Ever After)

Shelly Maypo Mysteries

Spring Fling (co-written with P. Mattern)

<u>Coming Soon:</u>

If The Shoe Fits: A Howlin' Good Fairytale Retelling

For Fangs Sake

Moongate Island Christmas Claim

The Dragon's Surprise

The Dragon's Dream

Bearing Gifts

Vampire Shield: Guardians of Chaos 6

Chickee and the Paparazzi: FUCN'A

The Wolf's Winter Wish: A Macconwood Pack Tale

The Hybrid Assassin

Tiger Rejected

The High Alpha Series

Hungry As A Pythin

Fire Witch

Asterion: Speed Dating with the Denizens of the Underworld

Excerpt from *Wolf Shield: Guardians of Chaos*

What a day! Fergie McAndrews headed towards the pick-up truck she'd borrowed from her roommate for work that morning.

Of course, the thirty-thousand dollar certified used luxury car she'd splurged on earlier in the year was in the shop. Again.

Just another in a long line of bad decisions. After leaving a perfectly good job for a startup company, she was laid off three weeks ago and had to borrow money from her parents to pay rent. Wasn't that humiliating?

"This is the last time, Ferg," her step-monster had said *after she'd Venmo'd the money to her.*

God forbid the mechanic call and tell her the car

was ready. She wouldn't be able to pick it up for another week. That was when she got her first paycheck from her newest gig at L-Corp. Not a startup, but an older company with new offices in Bayonne, which was only a half-hour commute.

But to commute, you needed a car. Fergie had no choice but to borrow the old pick-up from her best friend and roommate, Jessenia Banks. It wasn't like she needed the truck. She worked from home these days. Besides, Fergie promised to fill it up and have it washed.

She huffed out a breath. It'd been a really long day. A crappy one too. Fergie wanted to love her new job. Really, she did. But so far, it was the pits. If Fergie wanted to be a librarian, she would've been one.

Research was her jam. Well, when it was interesting. She had a knack for sniffing out information and compiling easy-to-read spreadsheets and time-lines. It wasn't the hard work that annoyed her. Her complaint was the content. The actual stuff her new boss had her looking up. It was beyond boring.

Why an enormous conglomerate like L-Corp needed old land surveys, cross-referenced with newspaper reports on accidents, crimes, etcetera.

She had no idea. She'd been at it for weeks now. So far, she'd researched six locations given via GPS coordinates across Hudson County. Her new boss wanted everything, every little insignificant piece of information she could dig up.

That was the easy part. It was the hassle of the actual job that really made her want to give up. Every day she had to drive to Bayonne to pick up her work laptop she'd dropped off the night before with all of that day's findings. Every single night they wiped her computer clean.

Like she was going to run away with the secrets of what happened on 2nd and Washington sixty-years ago. Can you say paranoid? Ugh.

Fergie had always looked forward to working for a huge global company. It was supposed to be her ticket out of the Garden State. Traveling the globe, seeing new things, visiting far-off places was always a secret dream of hers. Well, that, and having her own walk-in closet full of gorgeous designer shoes.

Best secret dream evah! In her opinion, anyway. What woman didn't love shoes? Fergie hummed as she daydreamed about rows and rows of Blahnik's, Jimmy Choo's, Garavani's, Ferragamo's, and her personal favorites, Louboutin's on every shelf!

Don't judge. Fergie wasn't shallow, she just liked pretty things. Haters gonna hate. But every time she ran across a thrift or second-chance store, she'd search high and low to see what they had. That was how she'd scored the pumps on her feet.

They made her feel good about herself. Being five-foot two-inches short with more curves than a racetrack, Fergie had had more than her fair share of self-esteem issues growing up. Alright, so she was chubby. She could admit that proudly now.

If everyone looked the same, the world would be one boring as hell place. Fergie liked herself perfectly fine these days, in spite of all the times her step-monster tried to make her diet growing up. So she liked food and shoes. Big deal.

She worked hard to feed and clothe herself, so as far as she was concerned, no one had a right to comment. So what if she wanted some excitement in her life? Fergie was aware she was better off than most, but what was wrong with having goals?

She'd spent a lot of time thinking about how a woman like her could have an adventure. Travelling was the only thing she could think of. Of course, she'd been hoping this job would be the answer to that. Even travelling for work was better than being stuck.

Sigh.

So far, her plans had fallen flat, but hey, at least she was earning a paycheck. Her new boss, Mr. Offner, might be a strange man, but he signed her checks, and that was enough for now. Fergie had never seen more than a glimpse of him. All of her instructions usually came via email.

Most of the time she was able to compile her research quickly, then she'd head back to the office to organize it into neat little spreadsheets, and finally, she'd hand it all in with her laptop. But not today.

Mr. Offner sent her an email detailing everything she could dig up on one of the oldest places on record in the county. Of course, land surveys that old, along with police reports, newspaper articles, deeds, and sales records were nowhere she could easily access them.

After wasting hours at both the court house and municipal building, Fergie had been directed to the *second* public library. Apparently anything over a hundred years old was filed away in the godforsaken place. She'd been shocked to find an entire room filled with musty old archives. And wouldn't you know it, there was no cell service and no internet access. Plus, their phone lines were down. She'd had to photograph each page using her cell. When she got home later, she would send those photos like a fax to her boss along with her spreadsheet. If she could manage that before collapsing into bed.

Excerpt from *Bound by Air*

Troy Waman looked down at his smartphone to the little red arrow blinking on his map app, indicating he had reached his destination. He frowned pensively before shaking his head.

"What a fucking shithole," he murmured to himself as he exited the nondescript black SUV his Station Master, Rex, had given him for the job.

"Try not to scratch it," the tough Bear shifter had said with a barely contained growl after their meeting the day before last. After a thousand years of waiting, The *Wardens of Terra* were being called to duty and this was Troy's first assignment.

It took him a day and a half to make his way to Shadowland, New York from the little suburb in Virginia Beach where his Station was located. There were dozens of them across the continental United States and even more overseas, though he'd rarely been out of the county himself.

Troy rolled his shoulders and exhaled. He was the first from his Station to be called to duty. A fact that left him both proud and humbled at the same time. He'd trained damn hard since he was a child waiting for such an opportunity. Now he had it, and it was almost too much to bear.

Fuck and damn. It's time Troy, get your ass in gear. That was all the sympathy he had for himself. Why the hell should he have any at all? Troy Waman was no tenderfoot normal. He was a Warden of Terra. He didn't need to remind himself of the honor and duty that went along with his position.

The *Wardens of Terra* were an ancient group of elite warriors. All of them Shifters. Identified in their youth and trained throughout their preternaturally long lives, they were guardians as well as fighters. *Station Masters* led teams of Wardens across the planet.

Though they'd been deactivated sometime in the last millennium, Wardens were born, chosen, and trained every day with the distinct knowledge that someday, they'd be called upon to defend the earth. That day was here.

Troy Waman had been trained as a Warden since before he learned how to spell the word. His heritage was a mix of Anglo and Native American. His father's blood was a mix of tribes including Algonquin, Lenape, Cherokee, and a few others. He hadn't stuck around long enough for anyone to learn the rest.

He supposed he could get a DNA test, but that might raise too many questions with the normals. Especially in this day of advanced technology in biogenetics.

Besides, it was quite common in today's world to find Native American peoples descended from multiple tribes. Troy Waman was uncommon for an entirely different reason. He was a Shifter, a special race of dual natured beings with one foot in the supernatural world and one in the human. Troy was a *Thunderbird Shifter* to be exact. Something unique even amongst Shifters.

He stretched his long, lithe body as he stepped away from the vehicle. It was already dark out despite it being fairly early in the evening. *Daylight savings my ass.* He sniffed the frigid air. The unusually high winds made the cold seem even more bitter. The street lamp stuttered on the corner, a rusty fence squeaked, and a black cat crossed the street, ducking under some parked cars. Troy's frown deepened.

It looked like the setting of a B-horror flick. All it needed was some half naked co-ed to run down the street with a masked bogeyman stalking behind her, traditional blood-coated knife in hand. *Oh yeah.* They might call it *Shadowland Nightmare* or something equally cheesy.

He stopped his musings and used his heightened senses to take in the downtrodden area around him. It would seem upstate New York wasn't all orchards and sprawling suburbs. He smirked as the "I love New York" song ran through his head. *Yeah, right.*

Apparently, parts of the Empire State were as fucked up as the street where he was born in Newark, New Jersey. He'd visited that shithole back when he was in his teens just out of curiosity. What a mistake that had been! He'd left almost as soon as he'd arrived. His extended family had been, shall we say, less than welcoming.

His gray-haired grandmother had screamed and crossed herself when he stepped over her threshold. He was what they called a *skin walker*. They feared and loathed him as something evil. Him evil? Like he was the motherfucker who knocked-up some unsuspecting normal and left her ass with a Shifter baby.

He was not evil, but he was something they did not understand. He'd been angry and ashamed that day. He'd crashed through his grandmother's kitchen to hitch a ride back down to his Station in Virginia Beach.

In his youth it was more like a military training camp, but it was all he knew of home. After all, it was where he'd lived his entire life. He'd made his peace and settled fully into his life there.

The incident with his grandmother had happened over a decade ago, when Troy had stolen his records out of Rex's office. Still, the memory remained fresh in his mind as if it were only yesterday. The fucked-up street where he was standing only brought back the painful reminder that he'd come from the same kind of squalor. *Fuck this*, he thought.

The pungent scent of despair washed over him. *Reminding him.* A young man with a hood pulled up over his head, eyed him from the street corner. *Drug dealer. Shadowland* indeed. It was an apt name for this shamble of a neighborhood.

The young man continued to stare until Troy allowed his beast to shine through. His golden eyes pinned the errant youth through the inky darkness of the night. Startled, the kid dropped the bag he was holding and ran down the alley.

Punk. Troy walked over and picked up what he had so hastily left behind. A couple of grams of crack cocaine and heroin, *probably cut with Fentanyl.* There were also various sized baggies full of what smelled like some below average marijuana and half-rotted psychedelic mushrooms.

Just your garden variety of illegal substances to be found on most street corners in neighborhoods like this one. *Fucking normals.* He frowned and dumped the still sealed contents down the closest storm drain. He sent a quick text to Rex earmarking the location.

Rex would make sure the local police department got an anonymous tip to retrieve the narcotics before someone got hurt. Recreational drug use, mainly the opioid epidemic, was wreaking havoc amongst the humans with more and more of them succumbing to their addictions.

It was troubling, but not Troy's problem. Shifters were extraordinarily hard to kill. Most human drugs had little to no effect on supernatural beings. *Normals,* he growled the thought, *such weak creatures.*

To be fair, Shifters had vices too. He just had little

experience with it. Cecil, a Station-mate of his, had an adrenaline addiction. He was always putting himself in dangerous situations, even during simple training exercises. Fernandez, a Jaguar Shifter, was always trying to get into some chick's pants. *Sex addict.* And he knew of others who channeled their energies into ways he considered to be mostly unproductive.

His opinion, for sure. He'd always been something of a loner by nature. There weren't many Thunderbird Shifters around. Hell, he was the only fucking one he knew of in this part of the world.

He didn't blame or judge his Station-mates for their proclivities. Most of the Shifters he knew had large appetites which included food, exercise, and sex.

Troy had certainly explored that part of him. He wasn't a man-whore or anything, but he'd had his share of women. None of them mattered to him. Just a means to satisfy the occasional itch.

Troy was determined to live his life as a Warden of Terra alone. He never expected to find anyone willing to share what was a potentially deadly existence.

Those who followed the Darkness and evil were always looking for ways to gain the upper hand and it was his job to stop them. The way he saw it, it was an honor and a duty to serve.

He shared this great responsibility with the entire organization. The core belief of the Wardens was based on one indisputable fact Shifters had walked the earth since the dawn of time, even before humankind; therefore, they were responsible for the well-being of the entire planet and all its inhabitants. Especially those who were inherently weaker. Mainly females and *normals*.

There were other supernaturals who believed humans, or normals as they referred to them, were a blight on the planet. Those creatures wished to destroy them and take over.

Demons, Dark Witches, and a whole plethora of evil beings sought the destruction of the normals and the world they lived in. *Idiots! Did they even realize if they destroyed the world, there would be nothing left? Where the fuck would they live?*

Of course, the supernatural world had many agencies that worked towards the common goal of saving the planet. The *Order of the Guardians,* for example, were responsible for policing the various factions of supernaturals.

Shifters generally tended to ally themselves with the Guardians. Sure, there were *bad* Shifters, but he'd never come across any willing to follow the Dark. Simply because most agreed the destruction of the world could not be allowed to happen.

Different Packs and Clans, etcetera, of course, had different ideas. Some wanted to remain secret, others wished to come out, and other still wanted to rule the weaker humans. It was a whole fucking thing, and they argued about regularly.

Troy didn't know from any of that. He spent little time in the human world. His efforts better spent making himself worthy of being a Warden. Training, exercise, and following orders. That's what Troy lived for, it was why he was chosen.

Thunderbird Shifters were very rare. *Special.* He scoffed at the stray thought. But no matter what way he looked at it, Troy was indeed unique. In more ways than one. He was born *marked* by the stars. A *Shifter of Terra.*

From infancy, he was told he carried the power of his sign within him. *Aquarius* ruled his destiny and it would aid him in the never-ending battle against the forces of darkness.

Every single Warden he knew was a Shifter like him. They were the fiercest warriors on the planet. Like many others throughout the last thousand years, Troy, *a Shifter child who was marked,* was taken from his parents and trained by his Station Master until the time when he would be called into use.

All that time, he thought, *and here I am.* He tried to ignore the pressure building inside of him. He felt anxious. His animal pressed against his psyche, comforting him with his presence.

The significance of the moment was not lost on him. The Wardens had waited a millennium to be called to act. *He* had been waiting his entire life.

"Do not fear the future, Troy," the Herald who had visited his Station said to him when he'd brought word that they had been activated, *"Your destiny awaits."*

Troy wondered if the old man referred to the Wardens finally being called to act, or if the elder spoke of yet another legend. Troy had been shocked to say the least when the Herald had entered their tidy little Station in Virginia Beach with his flowing white hair. After he told them the news, he turned to Troy and recited another old tale.

"Young Thunderbird, you are the first to return us to Terra. Do not doubt your worth. Your destiny has been written in the stars since before you were born, Troy Waman. Remember, a Warden discovers his true measure when his fated mate is thrust upon him."

Whatever the fuck that meant. Troy looked down at

his phone, then to the street sign on the corner, and finally, to the faded numbers painted on the mailbox in front of the ramble of a house his map app had brought him to.

Fuck, am I thinking? Fated mates are myths. Stories made up so orphaned Shifters would sleep through the night. He scoffed at the thought. Memories of tales the head nurse, Sr. Maria, had told him at the training camp he'd called home for years invaded his brain.

Memories were pesky things. Sometimes eternal, and always fucking portable. But he was no longer a child. *No more stories, Sister. Now, I act.*

"A thousand years we've waited, and I'm walking into a fucking scene from a bad episode of *Hoarders*," Troy shook his head and frowned at the decrepit house that sat a few hundred feet away from him.

It was cold as fuck outside and his leather jacket did little to warm him. Avian Shifters did not carry around the same bulk as other types of Shifters. He ran hotter than normals, but the single digit temperature froze him to the bone.

True, he wasn't beefy like some of his fellow Shifters, but he was just as incredibly strong, and he was wicked fast. Much stronger than any average male. He paused briefly gauging the atmosphere.

There was something off about the place. He scented *Magic* and something else. His Bird bristled beneath his skin. *Easy now.*

Lightning flashed in the darkened skies, allowing him to see the worn shingles, and cracked siding of the beaten-up colonial in greater detail. More than one window had been smashed and boarded up with cheap plywood.

If anything, it enhanced the creepy haunted house feel of the place. The porch sagged danger-ously. He wondered how the place had managed to not be condemned by the town. One thing was certain, it was an ugly little turd of a house.

Who the hell put gray siding on their house anyway? Maybe it wasn't always that color. Maybe the owner liked gray. *Whatever.* He couldn't give two shits about the siding.

His only concern was the increased supernatural activity in the area over the past two weeks. Ever since the owner, a *Mrs. Renalda Curosi*, passed away. *A haunting?*

A creaking sound floated up to his ears and he stilled his movements. The sound developed into more of a *moaning* noise. An unearthly wail. It grew louder as the lightning continued to flash in the sky.

Troy had never seen a ghost. True, there were a

lot of things in the universe he had never seen nor heard of, but that didn't make them any less real.

If ghosts were real, and they made noises, he imagined that pitiful wail was damn close to what it would sound like.

No such thing as ghosts. Yeah, well, most people had never heard of Shifters either. And yet, there he stood.

His Thunderbird shifted once more beneath his skin, the beast flexing his senses as the lightning in the air drew him to the surface. *No.* He told his other half. His human needed to be in control now. He walked across the street, keeping to the shadows.

Something was indeed off about the creepy old house. He inched further to the black door. The knocker was in the shape of a face or mask. No discernible features, just a vague impression of eyes, nose, and mouth. *Shadowland indeed.*

He listened with his enhanced hearing and frowned. There was a distinct voice somewhere beneath the moaning and creaking. A *female* voice. His curiosity was piqued.

From what he'd seen in her file, Mrs. Curosi was ninety-seven when she passed. Her closest living relative was a half-sister, a *Magdelena Kristos*, and she lived over three hours away in New Jersey. The half-sister was cut from Mrs. Curosi's will recently. She'd bequeathed her entire estate, house, bank account, and all her earthly belongings, to someone named *A. Kristos. Another sister? Maybe.*

Troy hadn't given it much thought until now. A crash sounded from inside the house. He perked up as the feminine voice he'd thought he'd heard earlier screamed in pain. *Time to act.*

"Are you fuckin' with me?"

"No, Randall, I assure you I am not fuckin' with you," Rafe Maccon eased his immense frame back into his oversized, black leather chair and narrowed his ice blue eyes at his Third and one of his oldest friends. How long had he known the man sitting in front of him?

Randall had come to Maccon City when Rafe was about ten, he looked the same then as he did now. Tall at six foot three inches, muscular, and more than a little intimidating to the Wolves under him with his long beard and equally long dark brown hair.

Rafe, however, was the Alpha. He was more amused than intimidated by his surly friend.

"A vacation?! What the fuck am I gonna do on a vacation? Come on, Rafe, this is bullshit!"

The door to Rafe's private office flew open and in strolled a very happy, very pregnant Charley Maccon, Rafe's wife. The Alpha's eyes glowed as they landed on his positively glowing mate. She wore a long, flowy dress. The shade was a pale-yellow color that, Randall admitted to himself, looked damn good with her creamy complexion and curly dark hair.

Their Alpha Female was quite something. There wasn't a Wolf Guard in the place who wouldn't lay down his/her life for her.

"Well, maybe you should consider a vacation to be a relaxing experience, Randy," she dropped a kiss on Randall's cheek and walked past him, over to her husband whom she kissed full on the mouth.

The way his Alpha's eyes homed in on her when she opened the door was nothing compared to the hungry gaze that followed her across the room.

Randall had noticed it took a while for Rafe to get used to his mate's habit of greeting everyone with a kiss or hug. Wolves were protective of their mates, but Randall thought his Alpha was doing an exceedingly good job of hiding his tension. Werewolves did not share very well.

Charley; however, had stood firm. That was the

way she was raised, and she wasn't going to change for any, how had she put it? Neanderthal brow-beating husband, regardless of how cute his ass was!

Randall had no direct knowledge if the "cute ass" statement was true or not. And he didn't want to know. He liked Charley though, had from the beginning. He was musically inclined and often took to one of the common rooms to strum his guitar or play a few keys on the piano.

C.D. Gorri is a USA Today Bestselling author of steamy paranormal romance and urban fantasy. She is the creator of the Grazi Kelly Universe.

Join her mailing list here: https://www.cdgorri.com/newsletter

An avid reader with a profound love for books and literature, when she is not writing or taking care of her family, she can usually be found with a book or tablet in hand. C.D. lives in her home state of New Jersey where many of her characters or stories are based. Her tales are fast paced yet detailed with satisfying conclusions.

If you enjoy powerful heroines and loyal heroes who face relatable problems in supernatural settings, journey into the Grazi Kelly Universe today. You will find sassy, curvy heroines and sexy, love-driven heroes who find their HEAs between the pages. Werewolves, Bears, Dragons, Tigers, Witches, Romani, Lynxes, Foxes, Thunderbirds, Vampires, and many more Shifters and supernatural creatures dwell within her worlds. The most important thing is every mate in this universe is fated, loyal, and true lovers always get their happily ever afters.

Want to know how it all began? Enter the Grazi Kelly Universe with Wolf Moon: A Grazi Kelly Novel or pick up Charley's Christmas Wolf and dive into the Macconwood Pack Novel Series today.

For a complete list of C.D. Gorri's books visit her website here:

https://www.cdgorri.com/complete-book-list/

Thank you and happy reading!

del mare alla stella,
    C.D. Gorri

Follow C.D. Gorri here:
    http://www.cdgorri.com

https://www.facebook.com/Cdgorribooks
https://www.bookbub.com/authors/c-d-gorri
https://twitter.com/cgor22
https://instagram.com/cdgorri/
https://www.goodreads.com/cdgorri
https://www.tiktok.com/@cdgorriauthor